## He wanted her—plain and simple

Without stopping to consider consequences, Jack opened his arms and Susan stepped inside his embrace. He held her close, too close. He could feel her heart beating against his chest, feel the warmth of her body pressed against his, the silky softness of her hair beneath his chin.

His thumb rode the lines of her neck and then tucked under her chin, tilting her face up until her lips were inches from his. Pink and moist. She parted them slightly, inviting, and he rushed in, taking her mouth with his.

The kiss was long and deep. Finally she pulled away and buried her head against his chest. He longed to hold her like this forever, ached to touch his lips to hers again.

Perspiration beaded on Jack's forehead. He'd crossed a line he never allowed himself to cross with someone pertinent to a case. But he'd never met anyone like Susan....

## ABOUT THE AUTHOR

Joanna Wayne loves holidays, especially Christmas. She delights in the music, the decorations, the food and most of all the smiles on her grandchildren's faces. That's why she counts herself lucky to live in New Orleans, a city that offers a multitude of Christmas festivities, from candlelight caroling in Jackson Square to a ride on a miniature train through the City Park's wonderland of twinkling lights. She hopes *All I Want for Christmas* captures the joys of the season for her readers while providing spine-tingling suspense and heartwarming romance. It's her Christmas card to her readers, and it carries wishes of joy for everyone. You can write to Joanna at P.O. Box 2851, Harvey, LA 70059-2851.

## Books by Joanna Wayne

### HARLEQUIN INTRIGUE

288—DEEP IN THE BAYOU
339—BEHIND THE MASK
389—EXTREME HEAT
444—FAMILY TIES
471—JODIE'S LITTLE SECRETS

# All I Want for Christmas
## Joanna Wayne

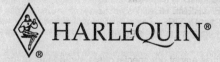

# HARLEQUIN®

TORONTO • NEW YORK • LONDON
AMSTERDAM • PARIS • SYDNEY • HAMBURG
STOCKHOLM • ATHENS • TOKYO • MILAN • MADRID
PRAGUE • WARSAW • BUDAPEST • AUCKLAND

To my children, Darlene and Russell, who never fail in
their support and love. And to Wayne always.

ISBN 0-373-22495-8

ALL I WANT FOR CHRISTMAS

Copyright © 1998 by Jo Ann Vest

This edition published by arrangement with Harlequin Books S.A.

**Printed in U.S.A.**

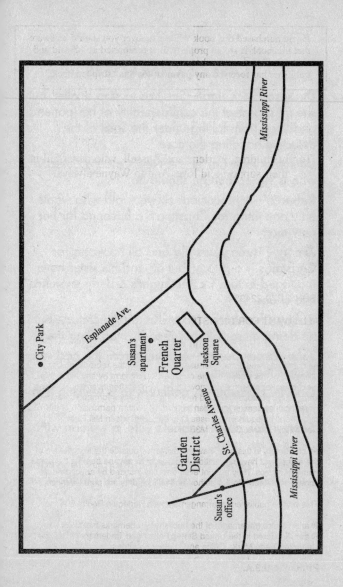

# CAST OF CHARACTERS

*Dr. Susan McKnight*—She has to stop a killer, but she must protect the confidentiality of her patients and keep from falling under the spell of the detective handling the case.

*Detective Jack Carter*—A New Orleans detective who is sexier than he should be.

*Rebecca*—A precocious six-year-old who wants only one thing for Christmas: a husband for her new mommy.

*Timmy*—Three years old and all he wants for Christmas is a puppy, but he and his sister have managed to turn Dr. McKnight's orderly existence into chaos.

*Bobby Chambers*—Dr. McKnight's secretary, but is he doing more with her records than filing them?

*John Jasper Darby*—A patient from the past who haunts the present.

*Gabriel Hornsby*—A patient who is walking a thin line of emotional control.

*Sherry Hornsby*—Gabriel's wife, a woman with plans of her own.

*Carolina Taylor*—She's been in therapy for years with Susan, but she just can't get her life together.

# *Prologue*

The man's gloved hands shook as he dabbed a spot of his cologne on the note. His signature. And he knew the good doctor would notice and remember.

Dr. Susan McKnight. Beautiful and destructive. The doctor who passed judgment, who changed people's lives with her words. He'd like to be a fly on the wall when she read this, love to see the sweat bead on her forehead, see that cool, calculating smile fade from her flawless face.

Crazy. That was what she thought of him, though she'd never put it quite so honestly. Well, she'd find out in the next few days just how smart he really was. Before Christmas, she'd know that he was not crazy but genuinely evil. There was a big difference.

"Stop me, Dr. McKnight, if you can." He sealed the envelope with a damp sponge. Not even a smear of saliva for them to check.

Crazy. Crazy like a fox. Dr. Susan McKnight had her work cut out for her. But she'd have to work fast. Three strikes and then *she'd* be out. Laughing to himself, he stuffed the sealed envelope into a plastic bag.

Strike one was already history.

# Chapter One

There were still ten days until Christmas, but the madness had already begun. Susan McKnight could read it in the anxiety-ridden eyes of her patients, hear it in their shaky voices, sense it in the tension that hovered over them like thunderclouds. The same way she could read the signs in every movement of the young woman who sat in front of her, wringing her hands and staring at the muted shades of green in the Berber carpet.

"I just hope I can make it through another Christmas with Gregory. If he were ever at home, it would be different, but since he was named CEO, he cares a lot more about the business than he does me."

"Do you care about him, Carolina?"

"I don't know. I think so." She shrugged. "I wasn't going to tell you this, but for what all this therapy is costing me I could travel to Europe. I might as well level with you."

Susan flashed a reassuring smile though she doubted Carolina ever told the whole truth. She picked and chose what suited her and then forgot what she'd said. Her stories seldom matched from one visit to the next.

"What is it you'd like to tell me?"

"It's not that I'd *like* to tell you. I just think that I should. I'm seeing someone else."

"You mean as in seeing someone intimately, an extramarital affair?"

"Yes. How do you feel about that?"

"How do *you* feel about it, Carolina?"

"I'm not proud of myself, if that's what you mean. I broke off with that tennis player last month the way I'd planned, but it's Christmas. I just can't seem to make it through the holidays on my own."

Susan kept her face poker-straight and her real opinion to herself. Her job was not to lay blame, but to help.

"You know, Dr. McKnight, I'd feel like I got more out of these sessions if you told me what to do instead of making me think for myself. If I could make good decisions on my own, I wouldn't need you."

"Only you can decide what's right for you, Carolina. The most I can do is help you understand why you do the things you do, and help you make the changes in your behavior that you want to make. I can't give you the answers because I don't have them."

At least not anymore. A Christmas ago, Susan had thought she had all the answers for everyone. Events of the past ten months had robbed her of that confidence, taken those notions of superiority and slammed them into the muddy Louisiana earth.

Still, she was the doctor. Helping patients cope was her job. If nothing else she should have learned *that* at the knee of the world-acclaimed Dr. Kelsey McKnight.

She forced her mind back to Carolina's problems.

"What is it that you expect to get from this new relationship?"

"I don't know."

"Would you be seeing this man if you didn't have the holidays to contend with?"

Susan kept asking questions, giving Carolina time to talk through her feelings. The young wife of a powerful CEO, she'd been in therapy for over a year, and her behavior patterns had hardly altered. Until she decided she wanted change, the sessions were a waste of time. Susan had told her as much before, but Carolina had an excess of both money and time, and she didn't want to be released.

"Just concentrate on what you need from the relationship and what you're willing to give. Then talk to Gregory. You might make this your best Christmas ever." At the end of their session, Susan walked with Carolina through the outer office and to the front door. "If you need me, call, and I'll work in an extra appointment. If not, I'll see you in two weeks."

"The week after Christmas. I have it in my appointment book."

"Good. Now remember what we discussed and try to make it a peaceful season. Don't set yourself up for disappointment."

Carolina stepped onto the wide porch. Twilight folded around her, the shadows from a towering oak playing on her face. "You need to lock this door when I leave," she said, her wide eyes sweeping the street and focusing on a man half a block away.

"I have an appointment arriving any minute," Susan assured her. "Besides, we've never had any trouble on this street."

"There's always a first time."

"I'll be fine. And careful. I promise." She stood at the door and watched Carolina hurry down the steps, her black pumps producing a rhythmic series of thuds against the painted wood. Then she turned her back on the gathering darkness and stepped back inside the cozy reception area.

She'd found this place by accident, passed it while searching for a neighborhood restaurant where she was to meet friends. The For Sale sign had lured her closer. The quaintness of the architectural design and the charm of the neighborhood had sunk the hook. A shotgun house, tall and narrow, in a tree-shaded neighborhood of turn-of-the-century homes.

That had been three years ago. She'd never been sorry for the purchase. Not only had the homey surroundings been beneficial in helping her patients relax, but the kitchen amenities suited her life-style. Especially with the type of daylight-to-dark hours she'd kept before the accident.

Before the accident.

Her heart constricted as painful memories forced themselves to the surface of her mind. Before her best friend in the whole world had lost her life in a fiery crash with an eighteen-wheeler. Before six-year-old Rebecca and three-year-old Timmy had arrived on her doorstep, heartbroken and confused.

Susan's fingers massaged a spot over her right temple. Before the two youngsters had turned her work-centered, orderly existence into pure chaos.

The phone jangled, interrupting her thoughts and jerking her back into the present. Probably her six-o'clock appointment calling to say he'd be late or maybe even to cancel, though Mark Bingham knew she expected cancellations at least twenty-four hours in advance.

She took the call in her office, cradling the receiver between her chin and shoulder while she picked up Carolina's records and headed toward the filing cabinet.

"Hello."

"Auntie Mom?" Susan recognized the voice at once. Rebecca had called her Miss Susan for the first few months she'd lived with her, then switched to Auntie. But Auntie Mom was new.

"What is it, Rebecca?"

"How come you answered the phone instead of your secretary?"

"My secretary gets off work at five o'clock."

"Why don't you get off work at five, too? Timmy and I are tired of staying with Miss Lucy. We want you."

"Because I have patients who need to see me after they leave work? And you know you love Miss Lucy."

"Well, tonight, I wish you were here."

"Is something the matter, Rebecca?"

"No, not exactly, but I need to ask you a question."

"Did you ask Miss Lucy if you could call me at work?"

"No, ma'am. I know I'm supposed to ask, but this is important."

"It's okay this time, but next time you should ask first."

"I know. We have rules about that. We have rules about *everything*."

Pangs of guilt attacked in the region near Susan's heart. Rebecca was right, and that was what hurt. She needed more flexibility with the children, but every time she tried, her attempts backfired. Habits of a lifetime were difficult to break.

"Never mind, Rebecca. You caught me at a good time. My next appointment is running late, so what is this important question?"

"Is Santa Claus real?"

Susan dropped into her leather chair. Gentle truth was the best way to answer children's questions. She'd preached that for years. Practicing what she preached was growing more difficult by the day. "We had this discussion on Saturday," she reminded her young charge.

"I know. Santa Claus represents the spirit of giving." She repeated Susan's words, mimicking her lecturing tone. "But is he a *real* spirit or an imaginary one? That's *my* question."

Susan swiveled to stare at the framed photograph of Rebecca and Timmy on her desk. She could all but see Rebecca's bottom lip pouting. Fortunately, the scraping of shoes on the front steps signaled the approach of Susan's six o'clock.

"This discussion will have to be tabled until I get home, Rebecca. This is not an emergency, and I have work to do. My patient's here now."

"Okay, but I don't see why we have to talk about it at the table."

"Tabling a discussion doesn't mean… Never mind, Rebecca. We'll talk when I get there."

"Okay, but Missy Sippen saw Santa Claus with her own eyes when he was putting toys under her tree last year. Now can a spirit do that or not?"

"We'll talk about it when I get home," she repeated, more firmly than she'd intended.

"Okay, but can I watch *Beauty and the Beast?* I know

you said I could only watch TV for one hour after school, but I didn't use my hour. I just watched while Timmy was looking at "Sesame Street." I don't think that should count. Do you?''

By the time Susan hung up the phone, she was twisting a tissue into shreds. "I am the adult. Rebecca is the child." She chanted to the plaster bust of Freud a friend had given her when she'd opened her first office. Freud was probably laughing at the doctor who had answers for everyone's problems except her own, but at least he had the good manners to keep his plaster mouth shut.

Her gaze swept to the door. Funny, she could have sworn she'd heard footsteps. Must have been the wind, she decided, picking up her appointment book and looking over the next day's schedule.

A first-time patient at nine and a court-ordered family study at three-thirty. Even lunch wasn't free. She'd agreed to a speaking engagement on "The Perils of Unrealistic Holiday Expectations." Tomorrow would be another long day.

Taking a small mirror from the makeup bag inside her desk drawer, she checked her image. Every hair was still in place. Pulled up in a neat knot, the simple coif was easy to keep and looked professional. Best of all, it made her look a little older than her thirty-three years. All the world craved youth, but not in their psychologist.

The door opened, and she slid her mirror back inside the flowered makeup bag as Mr. Bingham barged through the front door and stamped inside.

"Sorry I'm late," he barked, shrugging out of a dark blue suit jacket and tossing it across the flowered couch in her office. "Nothing I could do about it. Got behind a fender-bender. People in this town drive like a bunch of morons." Anger flashed in his eyes, as he spoke.

Susan took it all in with an expert eye. The man had missed out on a major promotion because of his temper, and his wife was threatening divorce. Pack up and move out or go for counseling, her ultimatum.

"Why don't you sit down, Mr. Bingham. That way we can make the most of the time we have left."

"Yeah. I'm paying big bucks for the privilege. I might as well vent about something more important than traffic." He poked an envelope at her as he dropped into one of the two upholstered chairs that cuddled up to a round table. "I found this by your door. Stuck under the mat. Obviously from some jerk too cheap to pay thirty-two cents for a stamp."

Susan took the envelope. Her name was typed on the front. Just a name, no address and nothing to indicate who had sent it. She tucked it inside her desk.

She took the chair opposite Bingham's and opened with a question. And for the next fifty minutes she listened as the man lambasted everyone from his wife to the President of the United States. His anger ran so deep it would take a bulldozer to unearth the source. A bulldozer or many tough sessions. Susan was sorry she had only the latter to offer.

IT WAS TEN MINUTES after seven by the time Susan all but pushed Mark Bingham out the door and into the first scattered drops of a thunderstorm that had been threatening all afternoon. A cool front was pushing though, but if it lowered the temperature into the fifties, they would be lucky. Summer, and unbelievable humidity, had lingered into fall, staying long past its welcome, as grating on the nerves as an out-of-work uncle.

Susan grabbed her coat from the hanger in the front closet and hurried back to her office to retrieve her handbag and briefcase. Sliding the desk drawer open, she rummaged for her keys. Her fingers brushed the envelope Mark Bingham had delivered. She stuffed it into the side pocket of her handbag and then pulled it out again.

She had several patients balancing precariously on the thin edge of control. If this was a cry for help, she needed to check it out here at the office, where all of the phone numbers were at her fingertips. A quick slice with the sharp edge of her silver letter opener, and a slip of carefully folded notebook paper fell into her hand.

The message was typed. She scanned it and then sank into her chair, her stomach twisting into a tight knot. She read the words again.

Dr. McKnight,
Happy Holidays!
Your first surprise can be found in a vacant lot in Algiers. It is the body of a young woman. There will be more to follow. By Christmas you will be begging for mercy. I will show you the same mercy you showed me.

Sweet dreams, doctor.

The grisly images the letter painted ran through Susan's mind like a nightmare in slow motion. Fingers trembling, she folded the sheet of paper and slid it back inside the envelope.

Who could have sent the message? Who was sick enough to think such insane thoughts? Did one of her patients suffer from inner torments so destructive they could drive him or her to murder?

Or had someone written this letter to punish her for some reason only the writer knew? She clutched at that thought, needing to believe the letter was no more than an idle threat.

But the images persisted. For all she knew, the man who wrote it could be out there now, standing in the dark shadows.

A shudder traveled her spine. All of a sudden she wanted to escape the isolation of her office. She had to call the police, but she could do it from the safety of her car. Hands trembling, she placed the note in the envelope inside her briefcase and headed for her car.

She jumped in the driver's seat, started the car and backed the gray Lexus sedan out of her parking place and turned left, toward Prytania street. The rain had intensified, pelting her windshield in sheets. One hand on the wheel, she dialed 911 on her cellular phone and waited to be connected with the police.

"GIVE ME A HIGH FIVE, podner." Jack Carter's voice boomed and echoed down the walls of Children's Hospital.

He moved on to the next bed. "Ho, ho, ho. And what do you want for Christmas, Matilda?"

A petite brunette in a hospital gown grinned and stared at him, reaching a bandaged arm to run her swollen and bruised fingers through his fake gray beard. "How did you know my name?" she asked, wonder shining in her dark eyes.

"Because I'm Santa Claus." And because it was written on her wristband. He kept that fact to himself. Even Santa had to have a few secrets.

She giggled. "How did you know I was here?"

"Santa knows everything."

"Then how come you had to ask me what I want for Christmas?"

"I didn't." He reached into the canvas bag that was depleting quickly and came up with a Barbie doll in a shimmering red dress. "I picked this out especially for you."

"Oooooh. She's so pretty." She trailed her fingers along the hem of the doll's skirt. "Can I keep her and take her home with me?"

"She's yours. If you don't take her home, I imagine she'll be pretty upset with you."

"My momma said Santa might not come this year because we have so many hospital bills. I fell from the tip-top of a tree in my backyard and broke my bones in seven places. But I knew you'd come. I just didn't know you'd come before Christmas."

"Old Santa visits hospitals early. That way you get a head start on Christmas fun."

Matilda wound her good arm around Jack's neck. He chucked her under the chin just as the beeper at his waist began its vibrating dance. He'd left his police radio in the unmarked car in the parking lot. Somehow precinct bantering about apprehending suspects didn't quite match the aura of the red felt suit.

"Be a good girl, and stay out of those trees, Matilda."

She promised she would and settled into skipping her new doll across her pillow while Jack headed down the hall in search of a phone. One night without an emergency. An hour to spread a little cheer with a bunch of hospitalized kids. You'd think that wouldn't be too much to ask.

JACK SWERVED INTO the spot marked Tow Away Zone and straightened his red cap. The simplest thing would have been to finish his rounds at the hospital, change into street clothes and *then* make this call. But the Chief had insisted on a rush with this one. Dr. Susan Mc-Knight, a shrink with clout and a complaint. A dangerous combination.

He'd finish up fast and get back to the hospital. Besides, a Santa cop might make this woman's day. She could analyze his motives, evaluate his emotional stability and probably declare him unfit. She wouldn't be the first. The chief did that on a regular basis.

Of course, the rest of the time he was patting him on the back and giving out the next tough assignment, the kind the more conventional cops turned up their noses at. It's dirty and a little underhanded—give it to Jack Carter. He wondered why he'd drawn this call. And why the details had been so skimpy.

Jack rearranged his tummy stuffing as he covered the few steps to the wooden overhang and rang the bell. A shrill yell told him there was a kid in the house and that she had spied him through the peephole. This call might be more fun than he'd anticipated.

The door swung open, but the person standing inside was no kid. The greeter was female, definitely female. About five-seven, hair the color of peanut-butter fudge, piled on top of her head and tucked away with a pearl hairpiece. His gaze slid past her bedroom eyes, all the way to the black leather heels. The neat, tailored suit she wore did not disguise the curves that appeared in all the right places. She was definitely a looker.

"Solicitors are not allowed in this neighborhood."

And a personality that canceled out all of her physical attributes, Jack decided, as her cool voice split the air between them. "Is that why you called the police? To report unwanted solicitors?" He fished his badge from his pocket and flashed it in her face.

She scrutinized him as if he were a slimy specimen

she'd slid under a microscope. "No. I called the police over a very serious matter. I expected a serious response to my request, not a department store Santa in costume."

"Cops have to make a living, too. A little moonlighting pays the bills," he said, playing along with her mistaken assumption. It was always fun watching the high-and-mighty get agitated. "Now, if you'd invite me inside, I could hear your very serious complaint and quit wasting time. I left a long line of kids waiting at the department store."

"I'm sure you did."

"What you bring me, Santa?" A wide-eyed toddler pulled at the leg of his pants.

"Hello there, podner. Have you been a good boy?"

"Yes. I ate my peas, and I didn't mean to pull Rebecca's hair."

"Then you deserve a treat." He rattled the keys in his oversized pocket and rummaged until he located a couple of wrapped candy canes. He held them out for the boy and his sister.

"Are you really Santa?" The pigtailed youngster spoke this time, her stare similar to her mom's. Another doubting Thomas.

"He is not Santa, Rebecca. He's just a man in a Santa Claus suit, the same way you weren't really Cinderella when you dressed for Halloween."

"I felt like Cinderella."

"And I feel like Santa Claus," Jack agreed, enjoying the fire the comment brought to the eyes of the gorgeous dragon lady. "Especially when my reindeer aren't acting up."

"Can I see your reindeer?"

"You'd have to go with me to the North Pole. It's

too warm in New Orleans for reindeer, except on Christmas Eve, of course.''

The dragon lady shot him an icy stare. ''The funny-dressed man is here to discuss business with me, Rebecca. I want you and Timmy to sit on the sofa and watch *Beauty and the Beast*. We'll talk in the kitchen.''

''I don't want to watch *Beauty and the Beast*.''

''That's fine. Then watch one of your other movies.''

Jack waited and watched as Susan McKnight picked up the younger child and snuggled him in between two throw pillows. ''Be a good boy for me, Timmy. Watch TV with your sister, and I'll be back in a few minutes to bathe you.''

''No. Not time yet. I want to watch TV.''

''Right. First you can watch TV.''

''Can I sit in the kitchen with you?'' Rebecca asked. ''I won't interrupt or anything.''

''Rebecca, please, just watch TV with your brother. I need you to help me out with this.''

Rebecca's bottom lip dropped in a serious pout, but she obeyed, kicking off her shoes and climbing onto the sofa beside her brother. Jack followed Susan McKnight into a kitchen that smelled of spices and baked bread. Unlike the owner, the kitchen was warm and inviting. He took a chair at the wooden table. Susan leaned against the counter.

''So what is this problem you have that needs police assistance?''

''I received an unsigned note tonight, just before I left the office.'' A tinge of fear caught in her otherwise smooth voice and captured Jack's full attention.

''What kind of note?''

She opened her briefcase and took out an envelope. The tremble in her fingers was slight, but not so slight that it escaped Jack's attention. She shoved the envelope across the table.

He slipped out the note and read it, touching only the edges of the paper, careful not to smudge any possible fingerprints.

"No stamp. How was this delivered?"

"One of my patients found it outside the door to my office, tucked under the edge of the mat."

"Have you ever received anything like this before?"

"Of course not. I would have called the police if I had."

"So who was the patient that found it?"

"My patient log is confidential."

"Murder is serious business, Dr. McKnight."

"So is confidentiality. And I'm well aware of my professional responsibility to the police and my patients. I'll cooperate as much as I can, but the man who handed me the note isn't the one who wrote it."

"Are you telling me you know who wrote this note?"

"No, but earlier this evening, I was at my desk talking to Rebecca on the telephone. I thought I heard footsteps, but no one rang the bell. I decided it was just the wind, until my next patient found the note."

"You know your patients. Is one of them nuts enough to commit murder and blame it on you?"

"Nuts? I'm sure you mean mentally ill. But the answer is no. At least, I don't think so. I can't even imagine one of them capable of writing a note like this. I'm not sure this is from a patient."

She dropped to the chair opposite his, her hands twisting around a cloth napkin she'd lifted from the counter. So the woman wasn't really made of iron. His protective urges surfaced, rough and raw, the way he lived.

"We don't have a report of any bodies being found

in Algiers, Dr. McKnight. My guess is this is some kind of kook out to frighten you.''

''That's my guess, too. But we can't be sure. Hostility of this severity can escalate quickly.''

''Yeah, or as we low-life cops in Santa suits say, the man might blow like a cheap firecracker.''

She drummed long, red nails on the kitchen table. ''So I suggest you do something to stop him,'' she said, freezing him with a challenging stare, her temporary vulnerability buried in the strong lines of her face.

''I plan to. Do you have a plastic bag I can store the note in? I'd like to have it checked for fingerprints. I'll meet with you tomorrow at your office to discuss possible suspects.''

''You might note that it is scented,'' she said, ''with an unpleasant odor, some sort of men's cologne, I believe.'' She handed him the bag as the phone rang and she excused herself to answer it. Jack took the time to scribble a few notes.

*Complainant might be hiding something. Not at all talkative where her patients were concerned. Cool, reserved and a stickler for protocol.*

He stored his other observations in his mind. *The woman was a real looker. Enough to drive a sane man mad if the conditions were right.*

A shuffling of feet at the door caught his attention. The pigtailed cutie had wandered over to check on him.

''My auntie mom's talking on the phone.''

He stuck his pencil behind his ear. ''Your auntie mom?''

''That's what I call her, but she's not my real mom or my aunt. She's a guardian. That's a person who takes care of you when your parents can't.'' She inched closer.

"Auntie Mom's real nice most of the time, but she doesn't believe in Santa."

"Do tell."

"But I'm not sure if I believe or not." She rose up on tiptoe to whisper the confession in his ear.

"Then we'll keep this our secret."

She giggled and ran her finger through his beard. "I'd like having a secret Santa."

"Then I'm your man."

She crawled in his lap and looked him in the eye. "If you're the real Santa, I only want one thing for Christmas."

"What's that?"

"A husband for my auntie mom. Timmy and I are too much for her to handle by herself. I heard her say so when she didn't know I was listening. But if she had a husband, he could be our guardian, too, and they could keep us forever."

Susan strode back into the room, saving Jack from having to come up with an answer. A husband for the beautiful doctor. A piece of cake. All he'd have to do was find someone compatible. Attila the Hun came to mind.

THE RAIN HAD SLOWED to a steady drizzle by the time Jack left the McKnight house and climbed under the steering wheel of his Ford. He poked the key into the ignition, but instead of turning it, he pulled the letter from its plastic pouch and read it one more time.

The note had the potential for stirring the blood of anxious news reporters and sending the citizens of New Orleans and the surrounding area into a frenzy. No wonder the Chief himself had put a rush on it.

Dr. Susan McKnight was concerned the man in the

Santa Claus suit might not take her case seriously enough, which just showed she could be wrong, Jack thought.

The police radio rumbled, and he twirled the control knobs to kill the static. A carjacking at Tchoupitoulas and Magazine. Two patrol cars in pursuit. He revved the motor and pulled into traffic. He'd have to finish his hospital fun another night. Right now he had to get out of these clothes and into some less criminal-friendly garb.

He'd just turned onto Rampart when the real news of the evening hit the waves. The body of a young woman had been found in the woods off Behrman Highway in Algiers. She'd been strangled with a silk scarf.

A cold image of death cracked like a whip in Jack's head, spurring him into action. He yanked the portable flasher from the seat beside him and stuck it on the dashboard, the blue lights clearing the way as he sped through traffic. There was no time to waste on changing clothes. Santa Claus was on his way to the scene of the crime.

# *Chapter Two*

It was past two in the morning when Jack Carter finally climbed into the shower. He adjusted the temperature until the water was as hot as he could stand it, then stood under the spray.

Soap and steamy water would help, but it could not begin to remove the horror of what he had witnessed tonight. From Santa Claus to homicide in less than sixty minutes. All in a night's work for an NOPD detective, but he never got used to it.

And tonight was worse than most. Not that the murder scene was particularly grisly. If anything, it was clean. A simple murder. But the victim was way too young to die. She'd had her whole life ahead of her until someone decided he should be her executioner. He'd tied a silk scarf around her neck and squeezed until life had ebbed from her body.

A silk scarf. He hadn't even been imaginative. So now he had a murderous maniac to track down and arrest. Of course that might be easier than the task he'd have to face first thing in the morning. He'd have to greet Dr.

Susan McKnight with the news that the note she'd received tonight had probably not been a hoax.

The details were still swimming in Jack's mind as he dried himself and pulled on a pair of red flannel boxers. A female, Caucasian, looked to be in her mid-twenties. Sandy blond hair. Trim. Dressed in a business suit. And the one fact that rumbled in his mind from the moment he'd arrived on the scene. The victim had borne a startling resemblance to Dr. Susan McKnight.

Moving barefoot across the cold tile floors of his apartment, Jack walked to the kitchen and swung open the refrigerator door. Milk, beer or leftover pizza were his choices. He settled for a glass of milk and took it with him to bed.

He needed nourishment and sleep. First thing in the morning, he'd have to deal with the dragon lady. Somehow she held the key to the identity of the killer. And he intended to find it, before the crackpot continued adding his own twist to the tradition of holiday greetings.

*8:00 a.m.*

SUN PEEKED THROUGH the open blinds and the smell of fresh-brewed coffee floated on the air. Susan leaned over her desk, and perused the records in front of her.

"Don't you believe in locking doors?" The male voice cut the early-morning quiet.

Susan jerked to attention, knocking the stack of files at her elbow to the floor. She recognized the voice but not the man standing in the doorway of her office. The fat, graying Santa of the night before had shed his stuffed red suit in favor of jeans, a gray sweatshirt and a lean, fit body.

"Don't *you* believe in knocking?" she answered, reaching down to retrieve the nearest fallen files.

"My manners need work." His lips parted in a half smile that clearly stated his manners were the least of his worries. "Interesting filing system you have."

"Very funny, Detective Carter, but I'm sure you're here for something more important than to spread joviality and candy canes."

"You're right." He stepped inside and stooped to pick up the rest of the files that were scattered over the floor. "I'm fresh out of candy canes."

She bent on one knee and helped him. For a second, she thought she might have misjudged the man last night. A second later, she knew she hadn't. He was pausing to read the names on the labels. She took the folders from him and dropped them on top of a file cabinet.

The names and notes on the charts were confidential. In the wrong hands, the confessions of indiscretions and self-perceived sins she heard during therapeutic sessions could wreak havoc on the lives of her patients. And some of her patients had enemies who'd love to ruin them.

"The bigger they are, the harder they fall" was never truer than in the realms of politics and wealth. She had more than a few of the town's biggest in both areas, proving once again that wealth and power did not necessarily go hand in hand with happiness and emotional stability.

"Nice office you have here," Jack said, when she'd returned to her desk. His gaze took in the room, settling on the coffeepot and pottery mugs on a corner table. "Mind if I pour myself a cup?"

"Help yourself." She slid the file she'd been reviewing into the top drawer of her desk. "And then have a seat. I'm eager to hear what procedures you have in mind for finding out who sent the threatening note.'' She was determined to keep the conversation focused.

He set his cup on the back corner of her desk and pulled a chair close, taking a long drag of the strong New Orleans brew before he sat. The look on his face was not merry.

''I take it you didn't hear the news this morning.''

''No,'' she said, trying to read his expression. ''Should I have?''

''It wasn't good. Shortly after I left you last night, a young woman's body was discovered by a couple of teenagers who'd pulled off the road to neck.''

''Where?'' The question came out as a hoarse whisper.

''In a wooded area across from a golf course on Behrman Highway in Algiers. According to forensics, the time of death was about 3:00 p.m. She'd been strangled with a silk scarf and then apparently dumped. Prints indicated she'd been dragged to the spot where the kids found her.''

Susan's lungs constricted as if she'd been punched. ''Who was she?''

''Maggie Henderson. Do you know her?''

''Maggie Henderson.'' Susan ran the name and the statistics through her mind, but came up with nothing. ''I don't recognize the name.''

''Could she be one of your patients?''

Susan turned on her computer and went to her patient files, moving the mouse until she reached the spot where Henderson should have appeared. ''She's not a current patient. If she was a patient more than three years ago, she might not be on the computer yet. My secretary has just started databasing those records.''

"How about Maggie Latham? That was her maiden name."

Susan found the *L*s. "No Latham either. I'll have Bobby dig out the old records and see if there's a Maggie Henderson or Latham." She turned back to the detective. "So we know the note I received wasn't a hoax."

"We don't know anything for sure. Murders in and around New Orleans are nightly occurrences. It could be a coincidence."

"If you thought that you wouldn't be here at eight in the morning, would you, Detective?"

"Maybe I just like your company."

"Let's not play games."

"No, I wouldn't dream of it. I don't picture you as the game-playing sort, Doctor."

"Your intuition is on target. So why don't we get to the point of this visit? I have a very busy schedule today."

"Is what you have to do more important than apprehending a killer, more important than making sure he doesn't kill again?"

Susan looked away. Of course not. Nothing was. She was letting this man get to her again, the same way he had last night. She hadn't a clue why, except that she had the vague feeling he was switching roles with her. It seemed that he read something into every word she uttered.

"I'll do whatever I can to help, but I don't know what that would be. I lay awake most of the night running through my caseload in my mind. I can't imagine any of them taking someone's life."

"Everyone has the potential to become a killer, Doctor, if the situation's right. So all we do is decide who's in a situation that may have pushed him—or her—over the edge.''

"How do you suggest we do that?"

"We'll rate the potential of each of your patients. You might call it their ability-to-commit-murder quotient. Then I'll take it from there. I'll check out motivation, past criminal records, opportunity to commit the murder. All the variables I can cover.''

He leaned closer, his voice steady and persuasive. "You'll walk me through your findings, guiding me so that I don't misread the emotional signs. Together we have a good chance of stopping him before our killer strikes again, before another young woman loses her life.''

His gaze sought and engaged hers, and she shivered in unexplained anticipation. She and Jack, tracking a killer.

"All you have to do is give me access to your files.''

Susan shook her head, anger destroying the brief period of anticipation. So this was the game the detective had in mind. He'd make her feel the two of them were on the same team, entice her into unethical conduct.

"I'm afraid I can't do that, Detective. As I told you last night, my records are confidential.''

"Not when murder is involved. You have a legal duty to—''

"I'm *well* aware of my legal duties," she interrupted before he drove *her* over the edge. "If you have evidence that *one* of my patients is a suspect, I can accommodate you. But no judge in the country is going to grant you a subpoena to view *all* of my records. I'll go through the files today and select those patients with decidedly aggressive tendencies. Then we'll talk, if you're interested.''

"You're calling the shots. What time do you want me here?"

"Not here. We'll have to meet at my apartment. How about tonight at ten? Rebecca and Timmy will be in bed by then, and I'll have had time to put together a few profiles for you to look at."

"Ten it is. You make the coffee and I'll bring the doughnuts."

"This isn't a party."

"Absolutely not. If I even act as if I enjoy the doughnut, you snatch it from my hands and stuff it down the disposal." He gave a mock salute and disappeared through the door.

Susan swallowed and tossed the pen she'd been holding across the desk. The man was impossible. A typical know-it-all, manipulating, devilishly handsome cop. For two cents she'd call the chief of police and demand he be replaced as investigating detective on this case.

But then this was New Orleans. She might be exchanging the known devil for something worse. A sigh of frustration escaped her lips. A killer on the loose who'd made her a silent partner in his acts of violence and an investigating detective who had no regard for her ethical obligations.

This on top of anxiety-ridden patients and two children who needed all she could give and more. No wonder cold, bleak, *quiet* January was her favorite month of the year.

*11:45 p.m.*

SUSAN SLIPPED HER stockinged feet from the confining shoes. Stretching her legs beneath the kitchen table, she flexed and wiggled her toes. The big toe on her right foot brushed the leg of Jack Carter. She jerked away as if she'd rubbed it against broken glass.

"I don't bite," he said, looking up from the notes he'd had his nose buried in for the last half hour.

"I know. I'm just tired. It's nearly midnight and we've been sitting in this one spot for two hours."

"A couple more questions and I'll get out of here and let you get some rest."

"Why bother? You've had questions about everything I've shown you, and you're never satisfied with my answers."

Jack stared at her for long, silent seconds before speaking. "I'm not doing this to aggravate you. If there was a way to leave you out of this mess, I would."

The concern in his voice caught her off guard, and a strange fluttery sensation skittered along her nerve endings. It was the late hour, she told herself. Besides, so much time spent alone with an attractive man was bound to affect the senses. It meant absolutely nothing.

"Ask your questions," she said. She meant the words to come out cool and steady, but a tremor slipped in.

He picked up on it immediately. "I can ask these questions tomorrow if you're too tired."

"No. I'm fine."

"Okay." He pushed a page of her own notes in front of her. "Tell me a little more about this guy. You say here he's unusually jealous of his wife."

The muscles in Susan's stomach tightened. Gabriel Hornsby's past would make fascinating reading for the detective, but if it leaked out to the wrong people, it could have a very damaging effect on his life. She considered her words carefully.

"He's in his mid-fifties. His wife is twenty years younger and quite beautiful. She's out of town frequently on business, and he gets upset if he calls her hotel room at night and she doesn't answer.''

''Poor guy. Insanely jealous men should never marry.''

''I didn't say *insanely* jealous. I said unusually.''

''Right. So what about the wife? How does she handle it when he goes berserk?''

Susan twisted the napkin at her fingertips. She hadn't said the man was insanely jealous and she hadn't said he went berserk, but both descriptions were probably truer than her own. Still, they drew a false picture of Gabriel. ''His wife appears to be very caring, but she is becoming increasingly annoyed by his reactions. She bears the brunt of his insecurities even though they were formed at an early age, long before she came into the picture.''

Susan ran her fingers along the rim of her empty coffee cup. ''His actions may well cost him his marriage if he's not able to move past the obstacles and develop more mature patterns of coping.''

''So the poor slob needs to let up before his wife decides that if she's got the name she might as well play the game.''

''In a manner of speaking.''

''Yeah, well, I told you, I'm a simple man. Words of more than two syllables twist my tongue, but I speak fluent cop talk. So, what kind of work does this traveling babe do?''

Susan stared at Jack icily. He was doing it again, pulling her strings on purpose, trying to get her worked up so she'd slip and give more information than she intended. She slid her feet back into her shoes and sat up straight. ''The *lady* is an officer in one the area's largest banks.''

"And is she running around on him?"

"Not that I know of, but it's possible. I only know what my patient tells me. He's basing his jealousies on speculation."

"What about the husband? What are these deep dark secrets of the past that messed up his mind?" Jack picked up his coffee cup and swirled the dark liquid.

Susan thought for a minute, deciding how much she could say without revealing the man's identity and wrecking his life. "He witnessed the infidelity of his mother," she finally explained, "on many occasions— when he was a preteen."

A whistle and a low curse flew from Jack's lips. He set his cup on the table. "Sorry about the language. It just slipped out."

"No problem. I'm sure it's a standard exclamation in cop talk, being one syllable and simple."

"*Touché.* But that has to be tough on a kid, seeing something like that."

"It was, but actually *witnessed* was not the correct word. He was in the house and he was aware of what was going on. He didn't actually see anything."

"Still, that would have to mess up a boy's mind real good, carry over into adulthood. Might even drive a man to kill, if the situation was right."

"It might, but I don't believe so, not in this case."

Jack leaned in close. "I need his name, Susan. I have to check this one out."

Panic punched her in the stomach. This wasn't their man, and she couldn't give Jack his name. Not that she didn't want to find the killer. She wanted it at least as badly as Jack Carter did. All she'd been able to think about, the entire day, was the young woman, strangled, her life stolen from her. And somehow Susan was at the root of the murderer's insane behaviors.

But still she couldn't destroy an innocent man who'd trusted her, who'd believed her promise of confidentiality. Not when that man was Gabriel.

Gabriel Hornsby, prominent New Orleans surgeon, son of Marilyn Hornsby, state representative. One whisper of all of this and the newspapers would have a field day. One whisper and Marilyn's career would be destroyed. One whisper and Gabriel would regress to the point he'd been at two years ago when he'd first walked into her office.

Suddenly the odor of the half-eaten doughnut at her elbow was sickeningly sweet. She stood and carried it to the trash.

"His name, Susan. I need the man's name." Jack's voice was insistent. "You gave me two other names to check out. What makes this man so special?"

When had Jack switched from *Dr. McKnight* to *Susan?* No matter. It was just another ploy to win her confidence, to make her do something she knew was ethically and inherently wrong. She turned to face him. "I can't give you his name."

"For Pete's sake, a woman's dead. If you don't cooperate, I'll go to a judge and force you to release this man's records."

"Give me another choice, Detective."

"Another choice? What do you have in mind? Maybe you'd like to conduct the investigation yourself. Dr. Susan McKnight, Psychologist Policewoman."

She took a deep breath. "It's not what I'd like to do. It's what I have to do."

Jack jumped up, the kitchen chair scraping noisily behind him, his face twisted in aggravation. "I thought psychologists were the masters of reason. You are making no sense.''

"Lower your voice—you'll wake the children," she cautioned, her voice and emotions much more controlled than his. "Tell me what to do, detective. I can follow directions."

He walked over and stood in front of her, his body invading her space. "I've told you what to do. Give me the man's name. I'll check his whereabouts at the time of the murder."

"What if I can do that for you? We'll have the same results without my breaking confidentiality."

"You're not a police officer. I can't allow you to start questioning a murder suspect."

"Sure you can. If I'm not a police officer, I don't have to follow your rules. I don't need to issue a Miranda warning. I'll just ask a few questions and snoop around. If I find he has a proven alibi, we can dismiss him without ruining his life."

"I have no intention of ruining his life unless he's guilty."

Susan rubbed her fingers against her temples. Why was doing what was right so difficult? "Just give me a chance to find out if he has an alibi."

"And if he doesn't?"

"We'll talk again."

"And in the meantime, the killer may be picking out his next victim."

A cold shiver shook Susan's body. No matter what they did the killer could be picking out his next victim. "Detective, my doctoral thesis was on the personality characteristics of the criminally insane. I gathered that material while working in a facility where that population received therapy behind locked doors and barred windows.''

''Good, then you know what we're dealing with here.''

''A psychopath. And the patient in question isn't one. Besides, all I'm asking is a chance to see if he has an alibi,'' she repeated. ''If I can't do it, I'll give you his name.''

''I don't like it.''

''Neither do I, but it's the way I have to handle it. I want the killer caught, but I will not compromise innocent patients.'' She shuddered as cruel images marched through her mind. A woman's body, cold and wet, lifeless.

Jack touched a hand to her elbow. ''We'll find him,'' he said, apparently aware that she was lost in her own dark thoughts. ''Just be careful. That's all I ask.''

''I will.''

He stepped away. ''I guess I better get out of here so we can both get some sleep.'' Turning, he walked over and deposited his coffee cup in the sink. ''But don't think we're stopping here. I need a profile on every male patient you have. By tomorrow afternoon.''

''I'll do what I can. But my sitter has Friday afternoons off. You can meet me here at two. That way we can talk while Timmy is down for his nap and before Rebecca returns from school.''

''Two, it is.''

Susan went to the front door and unlocked it while Jack retrieved his light jacket from the back of the sofa. He followed her to the door but made no move to leave. ''I'll talk to you in the morning,'' he said, coming up behind her and stopping at her elbow. ''I want to know exactly how you plan to check out the alibi. And don't do anything without talking to me first.''

"You have my word, Detective Carter. Believe me. I have no intention of playing any dangerous games."

"Good."

She extended her hand. He took it, but he didn't shake it and didn't let go. "You can call me Jack, Carter, or even Santa, but 'Detective' sounds way too formal for a woman that I see first thing in the morning and last thing at night."

Susan trembled. It had happened again, the crazy tingle that danced through her body and left her weak. She looked up at him and for a second she thought he was going to kiss her. For a second she wished he would. But instead he let go of her hand and pushed through the door.

"Goodnight, Jack." Her voice was low, and the name came out sounding like an endearment. For the first time in a long time, she felt the heat of a blush on her skin.

He turned and smiled, and the warmth inside her heated up considerably. It had been way too long since she'd been with a man. That was the only possible reason a man like Jack Carter could awaken any kind of desire in her.

Still, she'd be careful in the future. She didn't want to give him any mistaken ideas. He was not her type. And even if he was, she wouldn't become involved. Dealing with Rebecca and Timmy and stopping a killer were more than enough complications for her to handle.

*Friday, December 17*
*12:10 p.m.*

SUSAN CHEWED her bottom lip and stared at the file that was open in front of her. So where had Gabriel Hornsby been on Wednesday, December 15, at approximately 3:00 p.m., the estimated time of Maggie Henderson's death?

Finding out had seemed such an easy task last night when she'd insisted the obstinate detective let her try. Now, after a morning of searching her overtaxed brain for ideas, Susan was still at a loss. How should she proceed?

She'd tried the obvious, calling under an assumed name and requesting a Wednesday afternoon appointment. If Gabriel was in his office on Wednesdays, she'd have had something to go on. He wasn't. According to the receptionist, Wednesdays were his afternoon off.

The doubts had surfaced then, suffocatingly strong. Had the brilliant surgeon left his office and driven away in his luxury car in search of a young woman to kill?

No, it was too bizarre. Gabriel was disturbed, but not a psychotic killer. She was certain he would have an alibi. The best way to find out would be to simply ask him where he'd been Wednesday afternoon.

She'd have her chance in about ten minutes. Gabriel had called an hour ago and asked for a change in his regular appointment time, explaining that he'd be out of town next Monday and he couldn't wait another week to talk. Apparently things were heating up at home.

She looked up as her secretary stuck his head through the door.

"Some prankster called while you were with your last patient. He wouldn't give his name, just said to tell you Santa needs to cancel his two o'clock appointment. He won't get through at the department store today until three. He said he'd come by your place then."

Irritation knotted in Susan's stomach. Fortunately, she

had little time to fume before the front door squeaked open and Gabriel Hornsby stepped inside.

"I hate to ask," Bobby said, lowering his voice so that it didn't carry to the front waiting room, "but would it be all right if I leave now? Since we're usually out of here by noon on Fridays, I asked my girlfriend for lunch."

"Linda? I thought you'd broken up with her."

"Yeah, well, we're seeing each other again, trying to work things out."

"Good for you. And, of course you can take off a little early. I'm leaving myself as soon as this session is over."

"Thanks. Have a nice weekend." With that he was out the door of her office and greeting Gabriel in the reception area.

Susan took a minute to get her thoughts together. No use to look over last week's session. She'd already examined all of Dr. Hornsby's records, searched them warily for any indication his paranoia had swung out of control.

*Play it cool,* she reminded herself, walking over to open the door and usher him inside. He was a man with serious problems. The questions of the day were how serious and where was he on Wednesday afternoon. She stopped and adjusted the thermostat. The office was suddenly icy cold.

## Chapter Three

The session with Gabriel was barely past the have-a-seat stage when the impeccably dressed surgeon exploded with his bad news. When he'd arrived home from work yesterday, his mansion on State Street had been virtually cleaned out. His wife had left him a bed, a TV and a few odd pieces of furniture she'd never liked. And a note saying she'd call when Gabriel had calmed down enough to talk rationally.

"Why don't you tell me what prompted this?" Susan said, looking Gabriel squarely in his dark, troubled eyes.

"There's not a lot to tell. I caught a plane to Chicago. I was going to surprise her but it was me who got the surprise." His nostrils flared in anger and his hands knotted into fists. "There was a man in her hotel room."

"A man?"

"Yeah. A young fellow half my age. Running around in one of those hotel robes. I couldn't believe it. I just stood there with my mouth open."

Susan jotted a few observations into her notebook. She'd never seen Gabriel as upset as he was now. "Okay, let me get this straight. You went to Chicago to surprise your wife with a visit. Or was it because you thought she might be with another man? And when you got there, your suspicions were confirmed.''

"No, I went there to surprise her. I told you that. I told *her* that.'' His voice rose emotionally. "She came up with some ridiculous story about her partner's reservations being fouled up and said he was planning to sleep on the couch in her suite.''

"But you didn't believe her?''

"I wasn't born yesterday. I'm not a fool and I won't be treated like one.''

"I suppose you told her that as well.''

"For starters.'' He clasped shaky fingers into a knot and burrowed them into his lap.

"Take a deep breath, Gabriel, and try to relax.'' Susan got up and walked to the table in the corner and poured a glass of cold water from the crystal pitcher. Without speaking, she set it on the table beside him.

His large hand wrapped around the glass, but he didn't pick it up. "I trusted her,'' he said.

Susan didn't point out that he was lying to himself and to her. He'd never trusted his wife. Eventually, he'd have to accept his responsibility in all of this, but right now she had to help him deal with the emotions that were tearing him apart.

"Have you talked to Sherry since the incident?''

"Yes. She called this morning.'' Gabriel leaned over, burying his head in his hands. When he looked up, his eyes had a glossy sheen. "She'll never take me back. I know it. She's in love with someone else.'' He unclasped his hands and beat a fist against his palm. "But he won't have her. I'll kill her before I'll lose her to another man.''

Susan's stomach turned inside out. She struggled for a deep breath as Jack's words screamed in her head.

*A patient over the edge. A firecracker ready to blow.*

Gabriel squirmed in his chair. "No, I didn't mean that," he said, as if reading the suspicion in Susan's face. "I could never hurt Sherry. No matter what she's done, I love her. But when I think of her with another man——"

Anger reddened his face and extended the veins in his neck and forehead, but tears glistened in his eyes.

Susan felt his pain. The past tortured Gabriel, filling him with insecurities, robbing him of the chance to be happy, the chance to have a normal relationship. But had it created a killer, one who could tie a scarf around the neck of an innocent woman and squeeze until the last breath escaped her body?

Susan's instincts shouted no. But her mind couldn't ignore the possibility. "When did you fly to Chicago?" she asked, praying his answer would be Wednesday afternoon.

"Tuesday night. I would have called you before this, but I went nuts for a while. I haven't been able to eat or sleep or even work since then. I had to cancel two operations scheduled for today."

Susan imagined Gabriel's unsteady hands wielding a scalpel, and shuddered at the thought. "I don't think you should try to work until your emotions are more settled, Gabriel."

"No, I couldn't." He got up and paced the office, finally stopping in front of the window that overlooked a wooden fence and the top of the house next door. "Have you ever gone crazy like that, Dr. McKnight, wanted to strike out at someone…at anyone who crosses your path?"

"I've been upset."

"Upset! What I feel is much more than upset." He turned, his gaze locking with hers. "Now I know how family members feel when someone they love dies while I'm operating on them. If there's no one else to blame, blame the doctor who did nothing to help.''

*Blame the doctor.* The words settled like lead in Susan's chest, and the walls of her office drew close around her. Like a cage with no way of escape. She struggled to calm her racing pulse so that she could think clearly.

Gabriel Hornsby was a respected surgeon. He had a few personal and emotional problems, but he was not a psychotic killer. He needed her help, not her fear. ''Sit down, Gabriel, and tell me what it was like for you when you saw the man in Sherry's room.''

''It hurt, deep inside me. I've never known such pain.'' He left the window and walked across the room. With one hand in his pocket, he reached out with the other to close and lock the office door.

Panic rushed through Susan's veins as the lock clicked into place. ''Open the door, Gabriel, and don't do anything foolish. No matter what's happened between you and Sherry, there's hope. We need to talk about it.''

''Of course, that's why I'm here. But all the same I'd like this door locked. I don't want that nosy secretary of yours to come strolling in on some pretense or another. I don't trust him. I'm not sure I trust you either, Dr. McKnight, not anymore.''

''What are you talking about?''

''You talked to Sherry. You must have known she was seeing another man, and yet you let me go on believing the problems were mine.''

''Come back and sit down,'' she said, her voice as calm as she could make it.

Instead he leaned against the closed door. ''I love Sherry, Dr. McKnight. I have to make her see that. You have to help me. You have to tell me everything.''

"I've been honest with you, Gabriel. Now sit back down and be honest with me." As soon as he moved, she walked over and unlocked the door, opening it a crack. "Why did you really fly to Chicago?"

"Okay, I'll level with you. A friend told me Sherry was seeing someone else."

Gabriel fell back into his story, and she let him vent for a few minutes before she interrupted. "Tell me, Gabriel, when did you return from Chicago?"

"Wednesday morning. I was on the first flight out. I had seen enough by then."

"And what did you do when you arrived back in New Orleans?"

"What does that have to do with anything? We're discussing the problems with my wife, problems you are supposed to be helping me solve."

She didn't give in. "What did you do Wednesday afternoon after you got off the plane?"

"I rode around for a while."

"By yourself?"

"Of course, by myself." He leaned closer. "You know, you're starting to sound more like a trial lawyer and less like a psychologist." His voice sounded almost threatening.

But he was right. And she didn't like what she'd discovered. She'd wanted to protect Gabriel, but he had made it impossible. At this point she had no choice but to give his name and at least part of his case information to Jack.

The remainder of the session was nonproductive. Gabriel was sullen and argumentative, and her mind was restless. She tried to picture the man in front of her as a cold-blooded killer. The image didn't jell.

She and Gabriel were both relieved when the session concluded.

"I trusted you with my past, my present and my future, Dr. McKnight. You let me down."

"I'm sorry you feel that way, Gabriel. But perhaps you'd be happier seeing a different psychologist. I can recommend one if you like, and if you provide a written request, I can forward your records to the therapist of your choice."

"No, from now on I'll take care of things *my* way. By Christmas, my problems will be settled, one way or another."

*By Christmas you'll be begging for mercy.*

The words from the note echoed in Susan's mind as Gabriel marched out the door. Strangled bodies, patients she suspected of murder, a detective who dressed like Santa Claus. Why wait for Christmas? She'd beg now if it would do any good.

*3:15 p.m.*

"MISSY SIPPEN SAID that if you don't get toys from Santa, you get a lump of coal. So my question is, if we don't believe in Santa, is he going to leave coal in our stocking? *And,*" Rebecca rolled her big blue eyes to make her point, "are we even going to hang stockings?"

Susan pushed back a loose wisp of hair. Her question was, Why didn't Missy Sippen's family move to the North Pole? She stooped and picked up the crumbs from a chocolate-chip cookie before collapsing to the couch.

"Of course you can hang a stocking on Christmas Eve, Rebecca. That is a charming Christmas tradition."

"Does charming mean stupid?"

"No, charming means delightful...pleasant."

"Good, huh?"

"Good," Susan agreed. "So, what did you study at school today?"

"Same old first-grade stuff. Reading and spelling and math." Rebecca plopped down on the sofa next to Susan. "I can spell Santa. Capital *S*, small *a-n-t-a*. And I wrote a story about Santa coming to our house the other night. My teacher loved it. She said I have a wonderful imagination. I guess that means I'm charming."

"It definitely means you're charming." Charming, sweet and inquisitive and almost more than Susan could handle. It wasn't surprising. Rebecca had spent her early years with a mother who was outgoing, spontaneous and full of fun. The complete opposite of her Auntie Mom.

The doorbell interrupted Susan's thoughts, and she jumped from the couch. It was about time the detective showed up. She glanced through the peephole. All she could see of the cop was the red Santa cap perched atop his mass of dark hair. She didn't try to hide her irritation as she opened the door.

Not that it mattered. Jack smiled and tipped his Santa hat as if she'd greeted him with a big smile. Rebecca and Timmy scooted past her, squealing with delight.

"Hi, Rebecca." Jack gave her a high five and then bent low and picked up Timmy as naturally as if he'd known him all his life. "And how are you, big boy?"

Timmy pulled the red felt hat from Jack's head and put it on his own, twisting his lips in a frown as the border of white fur fell over his eyes and tickled his nose.

"Where's your Santa suit?" Rebecca asked, giving Jack's jeans and sweatshirt a disapproving once-over.

"It's too hot for fur," he said, bending down to tweak her nose. "So I just wore the hat."

"And how are you, Dr. McKnight?"

"I'm not fine. Detective Carter and I have to talk," she said, taking Rebecca's hand and leading her to the living room. "I want you and Timmy to play quietly for a few minutes."

"But it's Friday," Rebecca protested. "That's our special day with you. You promised yesterday that we could go to the park this afternoon. I already have my skates ready to go."

"Go to the park. Go to the park. I'm gonna climb to the top of the slide and come zooooooooming down." Timmy accompanied his words with sound effects and body language to show exactly how he was going to descend from the slide.

Susan glanced at the clock on the mantel. It was already 3:30. By the time she finished her discussion with the detective, it would be too late to drive to Audubon Park and give the children any time to play before dark settled over the city.

Her annoyance with the detective intensified. If he'd met with her at two o'clock as she'd asked, it wouldn't have interfered with the quality time she tried to give the kids. She rubbed a spot just over her right temple where a nagging pain was digging into its favorite niche and threatening a long stay.

A killer was on the loose and had to be stopped, but that didn't change the fact that the children had needs.

"I have an idea," Jack announced, plopping Timmy down on the couch. "Why don't we have our talk at the park? While Timmy zoooooms and Rebecca skates, we can chat."

"Yes, yes, yes!" Rebecca chanted. "Can we, please?" She folded her hands in prayer position.

Susan shook her ahead. The whole idea of discussing

a murderer while watching the children play at the park was far too bizarre.

"I'm free the rest of the evening," Jack said.

Susan hoped that bit of information was not meant to sound enticing. If it was, he'd failed miserably. "I don't know what your night's plans have to do with trying to have a serious discussion at the park."

"We have a lot of details to cover." Jack explained. His voice was still nice and easy, but the gleam in his eyes had shadowed, hinting at the darkness that hid beneath his words. "I have questions that have to be answered. We can start now, but we may have to continue our meeting tonight after the children are in bed. So there's really no reason to spoil the kids' outing."

"Please, Auntie Mom, don't spoil our outing," Rebecca chimed in.

Susan gave in. She was outnumbered. Besides, she didn't want any more discussion in front of Rebecca or Timmy. They picked up on every nuance of conversations, and she couldn't let them be drawn into the terror that had somehow singled her out to play a part in this game of murder.

"Get your skates and sweater, Rebecca. And Timmy, you need to potty." She sighed. To think that ten months ago her afternoons off had been spent reading a novel, or traipsing through antique shops on Magazine Street.

She headed for Timmy's bedroom to search for the shoes Lucy had taken off him when she'd put him down for his afternoon nap. Jack followed her, watching while she got on her hands and knees and retrieved one of the shoes from under the bed.

"I hope you're not upset with me for suggesting we all go to the park together. I'm not so bad once you get to know me. If you'd give yourself half a chance, you might even have a little fun.''

"It will take more than a trip to the park to make my life *fun,* Detective. Someone was murdered Wednesday and the killer has promised there will be more, or have you forgotten that?''

"I don't forget anything, and I take my job seriously, Dr. McKnight.'' He moved into her space. "So get used to having me around. Until the case is solved, you'll see more of me than you do your own shadow. So, we can fight or we can work together. You make the call.''

Timmy half skipped, half slid into the bedroom where they were standing. Further discussion was impossible. Susan grabbed a sweater for herself and one for Timmy before following the threesome in front of her out the door.

LONG SHADOWS from gigantic oak trees danced along the edge of the walk and shaded the sandy area where Timmy and another boy about his size pushed their trucks and made motor noises. His initial burst of energy was finally exhausted from swinging, climbing and zooming down the slide, and he'd settled into quieter play.

Susan turned her eyes from him to the sidewalk where Rebecca, chatting with another pigtailed skater, rolled by.

"Cute kids, but they must keep you running,'' Jack admitted, brushing sand from his jeans.

"I told you the park would not be conducive to conversing.''

"You told me.'' He took her elbow and guided her to a nearby park bench. "But the kids looked so disappointed. And you look as if you could use a little fun in your life as well.''

"At a time like this, wasting time on fun seems almost inhumane.''

"At times like this, fun may be the only thing that makes sense.''

"That's a strange philosophy.''

"Not really.'' He dropped to the bench and motioned for Susan to sit beside him. "Homicide detectives deal with death every day. Some men give in to the depression. An unfortunate few have been known to eat a bullet. The rest of us fight it. Fun is a major weapon in the battle. Fun, and little things like laughter and smiles on children's faces.''

A gust of wind swept across Susan's face, bringing with it the scent of supper cooking in someone's kitchen. Little things. The things her mother had never lived to give her. The things Carrie could no longer give Rebecca and Timmy. The things Maggie Henderson would never give her children.

A feeling of emptiness welled up inside her. Her gaze scanned the play area and the sidewalk nervously until she spied both of the children. Rebecca waved, and a warmth seeped into the cold, empty crevices of her heart.

"We have to stop this madman, Jack, before he kills again.''

"So tell me about the alibi,'' Jack urged, turning to face her.

"If he has one, I couldn't get it out of him.''

"Then tell me everything. You can start with a name.''

They spent the next half hour discussing Gabriel and the day's session. Jack took only a few notes, but his gaze was so intense, Susan felt as if he were pulling the facts from her brain.

Finally, emotionally drained, she leaned against the back of the bench and hoped for a reprieve from Jack's endless questions. She didn't get it.

"Tell me about the year you worked with your father at the Potter-McKnight Mental Health and Research Center," he said, leaning closer. "You must have run into some real lulus there."

"You've done your homework."

"I can't play Santa all the time."

She ignored his attempt at humor. "It's been six years since I worked at the Center."

"Psychopaths have long memories."

Susan shivered, partly from the temperature, which had dropped as the sun sank lower in the sky, and partly from the memories the mention of the Center had awakened in her mind.

"I don't know how much I remember about individual patients from that time."

"I'm preparing a memory refresher for you—a computer printout of all the patients who were in the Center the year you were there, their names and diagnoses."

"And you want to go over that with me?"

"You've got it. Like I said, you'll get awfully tired of having me around if we don't solve Maggie Henderson's murder soon. Did you find out if she was ever a patient of yours?"

"She wasn't. So the connection has to lie somewhere else."

"Auntie Mom, my wheel's loose. Can you fix it?" Susan looked up as Rebecca limped toward her, one skate on, the other in her hand.

Jack reached for the skate, turning it upside down and giving the wobbly wheel a spin. "Looks like we'll need a wrench, Rebecca. Do you have one on you?"

"No." She giggled and batted her eyes at Jack. "But Santa should know how to fix skates."

"Not me. What do you think the elves are for?"

She giggled again, and Susan bit back a cutting comment. Jack was only playing, teasing Rebecca and making her laugh. So why did resentment gnaw at her? Maybe it was because he was so natural with them, did so easily what she couldn't do it all, no matter how hard she tried.

"Why don't you take your other skate off," Susan suggested, "and go and play with your brother? We'll be ready to go in a few minutes."

"Okay."

Jack bent and unbuckled it for her. She gave him a hug and ran off. A hug. She'd seen the man twice, and yet she'd hugged him as though he was a favorite uncle.

Rebecca had lived with Susan for months before she'd hugged her like that. And even now hugs were more of a formality than a spontaneous gesture. They were reserved for goodbyes, good-nights and special favors. Not removed skates.

"Auntie Mom. That's an interesting nickname," Jack commented, leaning back on the bench and propping his right ankle over his left knee.

"It's Rebecca's invention. I'm neither their mother nor their aunt."

"So I've been told."

"By whom?"

"Rebecca. The first time I met her she explained that you were her guardian. You seem to be doing a wonderful job with them."

"I try, but I wouldn't describe my attempts as wonderful," Susan admitted honestly. "They moved in ten months ago. Their mother was my best friend. She and their father were killed in a head-on collision on a dark, rainy highway. They died instantly. There were no other living relatives.'' The memory of the deaths touched her as always, reaching inside her and wringing her heart raw.

She sat quietly for a minute, lost in her own thoughts as the sun rode the horizon. The quiet was short-lived. Timmy grew tired of the toddler play area and started toward the big slide.

''I think it's zoom time again,'' Susan said.

Jack beat her to her feet and headed toward Timmy. Susan followed him, but she might as well have stayed seated for all she was needed. Timmy scrambled up the ladder like an expert and Jack caught him at the bottom of the slide. If she had to bet on who was having the most fun, she'd have put her money on the big kid in the Santa hat.

A boy at heart, a cop by choice. And judging from this afternoon, he was very good at both. She just hoped he was good enough at the latter. Someone's life depended on it.

*9:30 p.m.*

''YOU WILL BE BEGGING for mercy before Christmas.'' Jack bounced the quote around on his tongue. It mixed with the taste of beer and pizza and came out tasting no better.

''So what do you think, Casanova?'' He stared at his fellow detective across the top of the two half-empty beer bottles that sat between them. ''Do you think we have a hoax? Someone trying to kill Maggie Henderson and lay the suspicions elsewhere? Or do we have a genuine serial killer who's got it in for the doctor?''

"There's a chance, albeit an outside one, that the note and the murder are unrelated. It's not the first time we've found bodies in that particular area."

"A coincidence would be *way* outside. But that's the reason we're keeping the details of the strangling away from the media. If we get another note and it happens to mention a silk scarf, we know he's likely our man."

"The reporters will go ballistic if they find out there really is a serial killer and you knocked them out of a big story. Of course, they'll claim they're only protecting the rights of the citizens."

"Yeah, so what's new?"

"I'd say that for the time being, you're stuck with the dragon lady."

"Yeah." Jack nodded and took a long swallow of the cold brew. "She's not quite as formidable as I took her for at first, but she's no bundle of laughs. I promise you that. And she guards the secrets of her upscale patients like she was the mother bear and those were injured cubs."

"Do you think she's hiding something?"

"Not intentionally. But I think the answer to this guy's identity is hidden in those locked folders she has in her office."

"Get a search warrant." Casanova leaned back and watched as a tall, slender blond woman walked through the door. "And speaking of searches, I'd like to pat down that one."

"Don't you ever think of anything besides getting a woman in the sack?"

"When I have to." He turned his attention back to Jack. "So, about the search warrant?"

"Not a chance. No judge is going to force McKnight to release *every* record, not when the good doctor claims she's working with me on this." Jack used his finger to scoop a pile of pepperoni and cheese that had fallen from his pizza. He deposited it on top of the one remaining bite of crust and popped it into his mouth.

"Then what's your game plan?"

Jack chewed and swallowed. "I've just got to convince her to trust me."

"It'll never happen."

"And why not?"

Casanova downed the last of his beer. "Because you told me the woman was smart." He laughed at his own joke and turned away long enough to flash the blonde at the bar a smile. "One other question," he said, "before I move on to more interesting company."

"Shoot."

"How was Maggie Henderson connected to Susan McKnight?"

"That's still part of the puzzle. Maggie was an up-and-coming professional, younger than Susan, but she bore a striking resemblance to her. It could be this guy's anger is directed toward Susan McKnight and that he plans to choose victims who represent her in his mind. You know, professional women, attractive, maybe even intimidating the way Dr. McKnight is."

"So she intimidates you, does she?"

Casanova was smiling, in spite of the seriousness of the subject under discussion. Jack wasn't bothered by it. As he'd told Susan, if cops didn't keep their sense of humor, they'd drown in the mire.

"Dr. Susan McKnight would intimidate a Louisiana alligator," he admitted. "But I'm not worried. She likes me." He got up and slapped a couple of bills on the table. "She just doesn't know it yet."

"You're not getting hooked on this woman, are you?"

"Me? Hooked on the dragon lady? You've got to be kidding. She'd be more trouble than running out of beer on Mardi Gras."

"I'd never let a little thing like trouble keep me from a beautiful woman."

"And that's the difference between a smart man and a fool."

A quick goodbye and Jack was out the door, jogging the half block to his car in a steady drizzle.

He'd wanted to meet with Susan again tonight, question her about any possible links between her patients and the note. But she'd put him off until tomorrow morning when she could get a sitter for her young charges. He suspected it was because she needed more time to decide how little information she could get away with giving him.

The motor of his car purred at the twist of his key. He should have turned left off St. Charles Avenue, but he took a right instead. He'd like another look at Susan's office. This time he'd see it in the dark, the way the killer had two nights ago when he'd stepped onto her porch and slipped the note under her mat.

An evening rain shower delivered its first drops of moisture as Jack pulled up to the curb and stopped, two houses down from Susan's office. Large oak trees spread their near-leafless branches, creating a shadowy arch over the street. It was only a few minutes past ten, but already most of the houses on the block were dark, the only light on the street emanating from the watery glow of streetlights.

And the porch of Susan's office was the darkest on the block. No wonder. The streetlight in front of her place was out. Had that been a lucky break for the killer, the night he'd delivered the note, or had he made sure it was out? Jack put the car in gear and let it roll slowly forward, a thousand questions plaguing his mind. It wasn't until he was past Susan's place that he saw the light creeping under the blinds in the back room of her office.

He braked to a stop as a shadow moved inside, silhouetted against her window blind. As he watched, the dark shape crossed the window again. One thing for certain, the tall, broad-shouldered figure was not Susan. And he could think of no reason why anyone else would be rambling around her office at this time of night, unless the guest was up to no good.

Jack parked the car a few yards from the house. Gun drawn, he moved silently through the night, hoping that the man prowling through Susan's office was the man who'd strangled the life from Maggie Henderson.

If he was, they could turn out the lights. The killing party would be over.

# Chapter Four

Jack wiggled the knob on the front door. Unlocked. His brain switched to automatic, as he checked for signs the lock had been jimmied. There were none. Silently, he pushed the door open and slipped inside.

The light was off in the foyer and front room of the office, but the door leading to the next room was open a crack. The light spilled out over the carpet and glistened across the top of a well-polished desk.

He moved cautiously, scanning the shadows of the semi-darkened room. No side doors, no surprises. That was one of the nice things about these old shotgun houses, especially if you were a cop. They went straight back. A bullet entering the front door could exit the back, or so it was said. That was how the house design had gotten its name.

Jack crossed the reception area, stopping where he could peer through the crack and into the lighted room. A male, Caucasian, over six feet tall, average build. His mind took in the details. The suspect sat at a large mahogany desk, reading intently from pages that rested inside a legal-sized manila folder.

So Jack was not the only one interested in the contents of those forbidden files. Adrenaline shot through him as possibilities rushed his brain. And none of the possibilities were that Susan had given permission for the man in the tailored sports shirt and chino slacks to enter her office at night and read her precious confidential records.

Hand poised at the butt of his gun, Jack kicked the door, sending it crashing against the wall. "Police. Put your hands up and keep them there."

"Don't shoot!" The man jumped into the air, his eyes so wide they bumped into his brows. "Please, don't shoot."

"Give me one good reason not to." Jack flashed his badge and sized up the young man who had turned a ghostly shade of white.

"I work here," he said, his voice shaky, guilt plastered on his drawn face.

"At this time of the night?"

"I had to leave early today so I came in to catch up on a few things. I'm not doing anything wrong."

"Just a dedicated worker. But in case you're lying to me, spread your legs and put your hands on the wall behind you."

The man complied, and the pat-down revealed nothing except that the man had a smell of beer on his breath.

Hands outstretched, the suspect backed away from the wall and turned toward Jack, the color slowly returning to his face. "I can explain everything."

"So start talking," Jack said, his gaze scanning the room for anything unusual. Everything was in order except the third drawer of the file cabinet. It was open.

"My name is Bobby Chambers. I'm Dr. McKnight's secretary. Call her if you don't believe me."

Jack tumbled from his short-lived high. This guy probably did work here and was no more a killer than Jack was. Still, the man had some explaining to do. Sitting at the boss's desk reading private files on a Friday night didn't give the man a lot of credibility.

Jack reached for the phone.

"Wait." The man shuffled in place, his hands digging into his pockets and rattling his keys.

"Either you work for Dr. McKnight or you don't." Jack stepped closer. "Make up your mind, and make it up fast. I'm not a patient man. Besides, we have a couple of empty cells tonight and the chief hates wasting the space."

"I work for her, but I...uh...I'd hate for you to wake her. She goes to bed early. Besides, I have identification on me and I have a key to the office." He pulled his key ring from his pocket and chose one from the dangling assortment, poking it at Jack. "And I have a plaque on my desk with my name on it. I'll show it to you." He turned and took a step toward the front office.

"Not so fast. I'll take a look at that identification first."

Bobby pulled out a leather wallet and handed it to Jack. "My driver's license is on top, and my gym card's right underneath it. Both of them have my picture."

Jack gave them a fast once-over, satisfying himself that the man was who he said he was. And he didn't need to see the plaque on the man's desk to know that Bobby Chambers worked for Dr. McKnight.

He'd already checked him out, and his record was squeaky clean. All part of a good cop's job. But Mr. Chambers's late-night office hours were still suspect.

Jack returned the wallet and picked up the two files that were spread open on the desk. Gabriel Hornsby and Carolina Taylor. A low whistle escaped Jack's lips. Speak of the devil. The very suspect Susan had discussed with him, but she'd been stingy on facts. Now they were all in his hands.

Jack's conscience stabbed him in the gut. He ignored it. Snooping might be unethical in Susan McKnight's book, but somewhere on the streets tonight was a man who'd killed before and had vowed he'd do it again. The next victim's life might be measured in hours. Or seconds.

Jack dropped Gabriel Hornsby's file to the desk.

"Those records are confidential," Bobby said timidly.

"So what were you doing with them?"

"Databasing. To tell you the truth, I had a fight with my girlfriend tonight. I didn't want to go home alone, so I decided to work a while, catch up on a few things. I'm working on a project for Dr. McKnight, getting old records together."

That might all be true, but Gabriel Hornsby's last record was from today, so it didn't quite fit into Jack's conception of "old." Jack managed an understanding façade, playing the game in expert fashion, pretending mild interest while digging for information. "A fight with your girlfriend, huh. Women. If it didn't take two to tango, I'd give them up myself."

"I'd prefer not to give this one up."

"When it's someone special, it makes it tough, all right. Was this a relationship-killer fight you had or just one of those kiss-and-make-up-later affairs?"

"Hopefully the latter."

"Yeah. Send her some flowers. That usually works." Jack made small talk while he flipped through the pages of Carolina Taylor's folder. Married to Gregory Taylor. *The* Gregory Taylor, CEO of Taylor Industries, wealthy workaholic, never home. Jack scanned the latest entries in her file.

Evidently Carolina had developed other interests to entertain her in her husband's absence. Young men, several of them, one a particular problem. He was Gregory's younger brother. The last entry was dated December 15.

"Dr. McKnight would be extremely upset if she knew you'd read that file."

"Would she? Why don't you call and tell her we're here? We'll see how upset she is."

Bobby made no move toward the phone. Jack was not surprised. His story about working here was obviously true, but he wasn't too eager to let the dragon lady know he was spending his evenings perusing files that read like the soaps and starred the faces from the *Times-Picayune* society pages.

Bobby picked up Carolina Taylor's file as soon as Jack put it down. He carried it to the open cabinet and slid it into place. "There's no reason to wake Dr. McKnight tonight, or even to mention any of this as far as I can see. You're doing your job, and I'm doing mine. And she has enough on her mind. Hopefully someone finds that lunatic who's tormenting her before he kills again."

"Did she tell you about that?"

"Yes. Does that surprise you?"

Actually it did, but Jack wasn't sure why, except that he'd asked her to keep a lid on this. One leak and the media would spread the news of a possible serial killer like mayonnaise on an oyster po'boy, and the perp would probably stop forecasting his intentions.

And that would be a major disaster. Without the link between the killer and Susan McKnight, it might be impossible to stop the murders.

"Do you have any decent leads, officer?"

"Information about the murder is confidential, Chambers, just like the doctor's files."

"Dr. McKnight trusts me implicitly. She warned me to be on the lookout for anyone snooping around the office. At the time, I had no idea she meant the police."

"No, but since we're both here and since you're already in on privileged information, why don't we have a talk?"

"It would be a waste of time. I haven't any idea who would do such a thing. I mean I hardly know Dr. McKnight's patients, but I can't imagine any of them taking a life, unless it was their own."

"Well, let's just chat anyway, seeing as how neither one of us is in a hurry to go home alone."

Bobby took a seat in a chair opposite Susan's desk. Jack took the doctor's place of honor. He grilled the secretary for over an hour and got exactly nowhere. No unusually irate patients that he'd noticed, no one calling or coming by on suspicious business, at least nothing Chambers chose to mention.

And Jack had no reason to suspect Chambers himself of anything more than unprofessional curiosity. He'd stopped to read a couple of patient histories before he filed them away. Probably no more than a thousand secretaries in the New Orleans area did every day.

Jack let Chambers leave. A couple of hours and dozens of files later, he left himself. The rain had stopped but water dripped from the branches of the oaks, the light drops rolling from Jack's hair and into his eyes. He dabbed at his brow with a handkerchief from his back pocket.

The handkerchief smelled of peppermint, leftover fragrance from wiping Timmy's sticky hands when he'd finished the candy cane Jack had given him.

His mind drifted back to the afternoon at the park. Timmy and Rebecca were great kids, but the doctor had a hard time relaxing enough to enjoy them. If the woman didn't let up, she'd drive herself and them nuts.

Rebecca had hit the nail on the head the first night he'd met her. Dr. McKnight needed a husband. In fact, he'd never seen a woman who needed a man more.

Someone to relieve her of a little of the responsibility that weighed so heavily on her shoulders. Someone to teach her that life was to be lived, not analyzed. Someone to make love to her, to bring that luscious body to life and have her moaning with delight.

His body responded to the thought, coming alive when it should be gearing down for the night. Gritting his teeth, he climbed into his car and gunned the engine. No way would he let himself even think of getting personally involved with Susan McKnight. The woman would chew him up and spit him out like so much grit.

A twist of a knob and the car radio filled the air with a jazzed-up rendition of "Jingle Bells." Jack sang along, letting loose with his strong baritone voice and adding a few drumbeats of his own, his large hand slapping the steering wheel. It didn't help. The image of Dr. Susan McKnight moaning in pleasure did not abate.

"Ho, ho, ho," he grumbled as the song faded to a commercial. The dragon lady and Santa Claus. Not a chance. Not even Disney could create a fantasy that would pair those two and make it believable. He'd be sure to keep that in mind when he showed up at the doctor's apartment in the morning.

*Saturday, December 18*
*4:00 a.m.*

SUSAN ROLLED OVER and kicked the covers to the foot of her bed. She'd slept soundly through the early part of the night, before a nightmare had cracked through the barriers of her consciousness. Now she was wide-awake, her mind rocking with frightening scenarios and a million terrifying questions.

Why had the killer chosen her to be his intermediary? Did he want to be caught and stopped, or did he merely want to torment her with his madness? Or was he mad at all? Could this be a calculating murderer, who craved notoriety for his deeds?

Kicking her legs over the side of the bed, Susan scooted her feet into a pair of terry slippers and pulled on a yellow kimono, a gift from one of her patients who'd recently traveled to Asia. Another man Detective Jack Carter might consider a suspect.

He had come to Susan at a point in his life when suicide had seemed the only option. She'd helped him through the worst of his depression. In the process, he'd fancied himself in love with her, a natural and frequently occurring part of the therapeutic process. Now he was emotionally healthy and engaged to be married.

Susan placed the teakettle on a stove burner. No matter that it was four in the morning. Sleep was over for the night, and she might as well go back to work on the list of possibilities she'd promised to have for Jack by 10:00 a.m.

She'd just poured a cup of tea and buttered a slice of toast when the doorbell rang. Her breath caught in her throat. Who could possibly be at her door at this time of the morning? She grabbed the phone, and started to dial 911.

But it was probably just a prankster, a late-night reveler walking home through the Quarter. But her mind didn't rest easy. If the bell rang again, she'd call the police.

The house was quiet, dark except for the kitchen, and her heart was pounding in her chest. It was the first time she could remember being this afraid in her own home. But Timmy and Rebecca were asleep in their rooms. She had them to think of now. And the man who'd left the note in her office, who'd murdered Maggie Henderson, could be standing at her door.

She waited for what seemed an eternity. The bell didn't ring again, and there were no sounds coming from the porch. She tiptoed through the dark foyer and peered out into the night. Her stoop was well-lighted. No lurking shadows, no hidden corners. There was no one there.

No one now, but someone had been there a minute ago. Fear balled in her stomach and tasted metallic on her tongue. *You will be begging for mercy before Christmas.* The words ran through her mind over and over.

Finally, she turned the key in the lock and opened the door. The corner of an envelope stuck out from under her mat. She reached out and grabbed it and then slammed and locked the door. Fingers shaking, she pulled the note from the envelope she walked back toward the lighted kitchen. And once more she read a message from a madman.

Dr. McKnight,
It's time for another Christmas surprise, something special I dreamed up for you. Strangling Maggie Henderson was such a delight that I've already chosen my next victim. She's a young woman who doesn't value relationships the way you do. Such a pity.
Happy Holidays

Susan read the note again as terror pummeled her insides. She wanted to cry, to beat her fists against the wall, to strike out at something, anything.

She didn't. As always, she bit back her tears and forced her emotions into submission. Steady and calm, a woman in control, she walked into the bedroom and fished Jack Carter's pager number from her handbag.

JACK SKIDDED TO A STOP at the corner of Decatur and St. Ann. It was 4:30 a.m., and the streets were quiet, though not deserted. People still strolled in front of Jackson Square and sipped café au lait at the Café Du Monde. He turned left on Ursulines, heading away from the Mississippi River and toward Susan's apartment.

He was running on less than four hours' sleep, but his heart was pumping ninety to nothing. He couldn't miss the anxiety in Susan's voice. Her attempt at control had lacked conviction. Not that he blamed her. He dealt with homicide cases every day, but this one was scaring the hell out of him.

Now note number two had been delivered. The man calling the shots had obviously toppled well over the edge. In this state he'd make mistakes. With a little time they could catch him. But for someone who didn't value relationships, time was running out.

And if Jack didn't stop the killer soon, time was also running out for Susan McKnight. He didn't need a note to tell him that. This man was seriously bound to Susan McKnight, even if only in his twisted mind. And he was bent on destruction.

Jack pulled up in front of Susan's apartment, jumped from the car and hurried up the walk. The second note had brought a new urgency to everything. The serial-killer task force had been alerted. They would be working hand in hand with Jack.

Now the Chief couldn't balk at the protection Jack had already ordered for Susan McKnight and the children. A police officer would be watching her house within the hour. The on-duty cop would know immediately if someone dropped off another note, and he'd be able to answer a call for help within seconds.

Best of all, this second note would surely convince Susan that she had to be more cooperative. Her charts on their own meant little to Jack. It was her expertise in reading them he needed.

She knew her patients and she had an extensive background of both academic research and practical work with psychopaths. Not to mention that she'd grown up with Dr. Kelsey McKnight, the acclaimed expert in the field.

She should be able to give him some solid leads about which patients to concentrate on. First she'd have to loosen her tight ideas about confidentiality though. He understood her position, or at least he was trying to. But frankly, he couldn't care less what skeletons rattled amidst the furs and Armani suits in Uptown's fancy closets.

His job was catching the bad guys, and if a few secrets escaped or a few toes got stepped on in the process, so be it.

Bruised toes healed. Dead bodies didn't.

He knocked softly on the door, avoiding the doorbell in the hope he wouldn't wake Rebecca and Timmy. That was the one thing he and the dragon lady did agree on. Those kids had been through enough without getting dragged into this mess.

The door opened and he barreled in. One look at Susan's expression and he was keenly aware of his early morning dishevelment. He hadn't tucked in his shirt or taken the time to shave. Susan McKnight, on the other hand, who should have been a mass of fluttering nerves, looked great. No makeup, but her hair was brushed into place as neat as a pin. Her face was scrubbed fresh, her nose and lips shiny.

A sweat suit hung loosely from her body, but it didn't hide the swell of her breasts or her tiny waist. And it wasn't knotty and scuzzy like the ones he usually wore on Saturday mornings. This one was the color of butterscotch drops, and the fabric was soft and cuddly, the kind that tempted children and weak men to sink their fingers into it.

"Hello, Jack. Thanks for getting here so quickly."

He tipped his baseball cap. "It's my job. Besides, I'm as anxious as you to stop this guy. The Chief is, too. He's moved this case to top priority." Actually he hadn't yet, but he would when Jack gave him all the facts.

"What does top priority mean in terms of handling the situation?"

"It means we don't have to haggle over resources—manpower or bucks. But it still needs to be kept hush-hush at this point. Not only would we panic half the town if the details leaked out, but it would make it a lot more difficult to catch the lunatic."

"I haven't breathed a word."

"Haven't you?"

She eyed him warily. "I'm sorry. I did tell one person, my secretary, Bobby Chambers. But he's as dependable as you or I. I felt it necessary that he keep his eyes and ears open for anything suspicious."

"I agree. You can't be too careful. Now, don't tell

another soul, even one as dependable as you or I." Jack tossed his cap to the sofa.

So she trusted Bobby implicitly. Would she if she knew he'd been in her office last night perusing the patient files? He'd have to tell her, of course, when the time was right, and that wasn't now. She might become a little hostile when she found out he'd perused a few dozen of the thicker files himself last night, and at this moment he needed her to be totally cooperative.

"I made coffee. Would you like a cup?"

"I'd love one." He followed her into the kitchen, and his gaze settled on the neatly stacked files and open notebook on the wooden table. "It looks like you've been hard at work."

"I couldn't sleep. I was in here going over files and making notes when... When the note was delivered." Her voice shook.

Jack walked over and took the empty cup from her trembling fingers. "Don't be embarrassed about being afraid of a man like this. You'd be crazy if you weren't."

"I'm not just afraid for me. I'm afraid for the next victim. And for Rebecca and Timmy. What's to keep him from breaking into the house to leave his notes? What's to keep him from getting to me through them?" Her hands clutched the edge of the counter.

Jack fought an unexpected urge to comfort her, to hold her against his broad chest, to whisper in her ear that it would be all right.

He held himself in check. Susan McKnight was not the kind of woman to cling to a man for support. One wrong move on his part, and she'd have him out the door and on the street before he could whistle "Jingle Bells."

He settled for pouring both of them cups of coffee and holding out a chair for her to sit in. "You and the children will have protection around the clock. And we *will* stop this man. He's desperate—he'll make a mistake. When he does, we'll nab him."

"How many women will have died by then?"

Jack took a long sip of the strong chicory-laden brew. Susan didn't expect an answer, and he didn't have one. What he had was a lot of questions of his own. They also had to take care of details. He had to talk to her about the necessity of tapping her phones at work and at home, and arrange a time for her to look through mug shots to see if any of New Orleans's known criminal element had been patients of hers.

Not bothering with niceties, he barged right into the nitty-gritty. "Who among your patients and friends doesn't value relationships?"

"The majority of my patients have problems with relationships."

"I can believe that. So do the majority of cops. What we need is a way to narrow this down. The man who's sending the notes obviously enjoys playing mind games," he said, toying with ideas out loud. "He's someone who prides himself on his intelligence. Which of your patients would that description fit?"

"Again, an overwhelming percentage of them. We have to have more to go on."

"It would help if we knew why the killer chose Maggie Henderson."

Susan pulled her chair closer to the table. "I don't have any record of having dealt with anyone by that name. Maggie is a total mystery to me. What were you able to learn today about Gabriel Hornsby? Does he have an alibi?"

"We're still working on that, going through the back door, so to speak. We have no grounds for questioning him at this point."

"So you got no farther than I did?"

"We will. Now, why don't we start with the names of patients who have quit coming to you lately because they didn't like your methods?"

Jack bombarded her with questions. After they covered every angle of the latest note and the clue the killer had provided, Jack went over his plans for tapping Susan's phones.

And just as Jack expected, every detail met with conflict. She welcomed having her home phone tapped, but her office was a different matter. They would have to install special equipment, which she would turn on only if she suspected the message might be valuable to the police.

She refused to tape her patients' conversations without letting them know they were being recorded. And if she let her patients know what was going on, they might as well splash the full story of their killer across the front page of the *Times-Picayune* or put it on the six-o'clock news.

Besides, as she pointed out, the madman hadn't called yet. His communications had all been written correspondence. By the time they were ready to switch gears and discuss mug shots, Jack felt as if he'd been in hand-to-hand combat with a heavyweight. But he had to admit he had a real appreciation for Susan's courage and tenacity.

Most of all he wondered just what the killer's previous contact with Susan had been. Why had he chosen her as his unwilling partner in this masterfully designed murder scheme?

"I need names, Susan, something to go on," he pleaded, stretching out in his chair. "I can't leave here without some help from you."

"We're on the wrong track. The killer is not one of my patients. I work with professionals, socialites, even a few sports figures. I'm not saying none of them would ever get angry enough to kill someone, but they're not psychopathic serial killers."

"How can you be so sure?"

"It's my job."

"So let's go back to your job when you worked for your father."

"I've thought about that a lot today. I did come into contact with dangerous psychopaths at that time. They were my father's favorite subjects."

"You mean patients."

"No, subjects. He studied them constantly. As far back as I can remember, he was fascinated by the criminal mind."

"That must have made for entertaining dinner conversation."

"We seldom had dinner conversations, entertaining or otherwise. My father worked long hours. I usually ate alone."

Susan stared out the back window and into a courtyard that was bordered by the brick walls of other buildings. Jack studied her profile. He'd give a lot to know what she was thinking right now. Whatever it was, it wasn't good.

Anxiety and lack of sleep had left their mark, deepening the laugh lines around her dark brown eyes. The dragon lady no longer looked her part. Vulnerable. That described her now. Softer, more touchable than she'd looked three nights ago when he'd shown up in his Santa suit.

"I know you think I'm difficult to deal with," she said, turning and looking into his eyes. "But I really do appreciate your coming over so quickly."

"No trouble." He did what he knew he shouldn't. He reached out and wrapped his hands around hers. She didn't pull away.

"I just feel so helpless. This man is calling out to me to stop him, but I can't."

"Not by yourself. That's why I'm here." He stroked her trembling fingers.

"It's more than that." Her voice dropped lower, until it was little more than a shaky whisper. "Somehow I'm to blame for this. These attacks are personal, directed at me for some wrong he thinks I've committed. But it's innocent women who'll lose their lives."

"Don't start thinking like that. It's not your fault, Susan." Jack eased from his chair and rounded the table. Placing his hands on her shoulders, he let his fingers dig into the fabric of her sweatshirt, massaging muscles so tense he could feel the knots that bound them. "You can't blame yourself for a man gone mad."

"Tell me about the woman he killed."

"I've told you about her."

"I know her name, address, age, profession and where she worked. All impersonal facts. I want to know about her, what she was like."

Jack hesitated. The other night Susan had asked few questions about the victim. At the time, he'd wondered why. Now it all made sense. The dragon lady was not nearly as tough as she seemed. That night she'd cowered behind her barricades. Today she was opening herself up to pain, because she thought she deserved it. And that it might help.

"Let it go for now, Susan. We can't help Maggie. We have to concentrate our efforts on making sure the man doesn't take another life."

Susan stood and turned to face him. "Just tell me—was she a mother?"

"She was separated from her husband. There were no children."

"Was she pretty?"

"Very pretty." Jack left it at that, omitting the explanation that Maggie Henderson strongly resembled Dr. Susan McKnight, and that she probably reminded the killer of the woman he wanted to punish. That he planned on killing Susan in the same way before this was all over.

Without stopping to consider consequences, Jack opened his arms and she stepped inside them. He held her close, too close. He could feel her heart beating against his chest, feel the warmth of her body pressed against his, feel the silky softness of her hair beneath his chin.

His thumb rode the lines of her neck and then tucked under her chin, tilting her face up until her lips were inches from his. Pink and moist. She parted them slightly, inviting, and he rushed in, taking her mouth with his.

The kiss was long and deep. Finally, she pulled away and buried her head against his chest. He longed to hold her like this forever, ached to touch his lips to hers again.

Damn, he wanted her. Plain and simple.

The room grew hot, as if the furnace had been cranked up to full blast. Perspiration beaded on Jack's forehead.

He'd crossed a line he never allowed himself to cross with someone pertinent to a case.

Not the touch. He'd held frightened women before, offered comfort when he could. But this was different. Even a fool like him knew that.

A stirring in the next room caught his attention. When he looked up, Timmy was standing by the door, dragging a teddy bear by the ear with one hand and rubbing his eyes with the other. Susan saw him at the same time, and she jerked from Jack's embrace as if they'd been caught in the act of making love.

"I'm hungry." Timmy toddled over to Susan.

"How about some pancakes?"

"With strawberries?"

"I'm out of strawberries. How about bananas?"

"Okay. Is Santa going to eat with us?"

"Not Santa, Timmy. Detective Carter. But he's welcome to stay if he'd like."

Her voice was cool and collected, and decidedly distant. A quick recovery, Jack decided. A minute ago she'd clung to him like red sauce to spaghetti. Now she referred to him in the third person and directed her gaze in the opposite direction.

Their brief bout with libidos was already exacting its toll. He deserved a swift kick in the pants, and if the Chief had any idea that he'd jeopardized the investigation with a kiss, he'd have made sure he got that and more.

"Please, Santa. Stay for breakfast."

"Detective Carter is his name, Timmy." Susan corrected the tyke again while she pulled the griddle from a shelf underneath the cabinet.

"I'll stay while your mother cooks your breakfast, but then I have to run. I've got work to do."

Timmy dragged in one toy after another for Jack to inspect and admire. Finally Susan set the boy's breakfast on the table. Jack stepped closer to Susan and lowered his voice so that only she heard his words. "Next time I see you, I'll have the printout with names from the Center. And hopefully you'll have come up with a name or two and some detailed information for me as well."

"Will you come back and play with me?" Timmy asked, kicking his feet against the chair.

"You bet. Is two o'clock all right, Susan?"

"If this is necessary."

"It is." He walked over and exchanged a high five with Timmy. "I'll see you later, podner!"

He cast one last look in Susan's direction as he departed. No doubt about it. He'd have to be on guard every second. The dragon lady had crawled under his skin in three short days. Go figure.

THE MAN STOOD in the shadows and watched the front door of Susan McKnight's apartment swing open and the detective walk out. He loved it. The two of them searching for him day and night, racking their brains, no doubt trying to learn his identity and his next move.

Crazy. Craaazy! So crazy, they'd never catch him even though he was right under their noses. Even though he watched every move Susan made. He'd tease her, torment her, take her through hell, the same way she had done with him. She'd pay a mere fraction of what he'd paid, but it would give him a great deal of satisfaction.

After that, he'd kill her. Sooner, if the web tightened. One hint that she and the detective were getting too close, and he was checking out of this town, leaving over Susan McKnight's dead body. Only then could he put all of this behind him and go on with his life.

Finally, he'd have his share of happy holidays.

## Chapter Five

Saturday, December 18
3:00 p.m.

"Auntie Mom, how do you spell *specially?*"

"Are you doing your homework? That's a long word for first grade."

"I'm writing a letter to Santa. I know he's only a spirit, but Missy Sippen says you still have to write a letter. She didn't write one last year, and she got the wrong kind of Barbie."

Susan put down her notes. "I don't think a letter to Santa is the same as a catalog order, Rebecca. The spirit of Christmas means you give and receive from the heart. Getting exactly what you want is not important."

"I know that. You told me already. But Missy Sippen says if Santa's going to come bumping down your chimney and let his reindeer poop on your roof, you might as well get what you want."

"Missy sounds like a real little sweetheart." And obviously a much better communicator than Susan was. When Rebecca had asked about the variety of red-suited, bearded, fat men she saw on a trip to the mall, Susan had told her the truth. In Susan's mind, it was the sensible thing to do.

Apparently Missy Sippen's folks didn't adhere to that philosophy, and Susan was beginning to wish she'd opted for the Christmas folktale as well.

"Do you think Santa brings things besides toys, if you ask him?" Rebecca chewed on the eraser end of her pencil.

"There are many types of gifts, Rebecca. Toys, clothes, musical instruments, food items."

"Yeah, but that's not what I want either."

Susan walked over to get a better view of Rebecca's handiwork. She was on her knees, using the coffee table for a desk. When she came closer, Rebecca grabbed her paper and hid it behind her back.

"I can't show you. It's a surprise."

"I think it would be all right with Santa if you showed me." Now she was playing the Santa game. She might as well. Rebecca clearly had no concept of "spirit." Reindeer poop was much more concrete and believable to a precocious six-year-old. Besides, Susan had no energy left for pursuing the argument.

"I can't show you. It would ruin the surprise."

"Okay. It's your secret." She only hoped Rebecca wouldn't be too disappointed on Christmas morning. More reason not to buy into the Santa fantasy. Susan turned and went back to the overstuffed chair in the corner. She needed to work while Timmy was down for his afternoon nap. She had several more patient profiles to chart, though she ran into nothing but dead ends.

"So how do I spell *specially?*" Rebecca asked, clearly irritated that she had to ask twice. "I want Santa to know I've been *specially* good."

"In that case, the word you need is *especially.*"

"*Especially,*" Rebecca repeated, mimicking her teacher's spelling-dictation tone. "I know how that starts. With an *s.*"

"It sounds that way, but actually it begins with an *e.*" Susan spelled the word and then went back to her notes. From Santa to a serial killer.

Depression settled about her like city smog. For the past ten months, life had consisted of one crisis after another as she'd tried to take on the role of instant mother. There had been nights when she'd come close to weeping from frustration and sadness, days when the responsibilities of caring for two children seemed more than she could handle.

Now, forced to deal with a killer, foster-motherhood seemed like a walk in the park. If she could just discover some clue to sink her teeth into.

She'd spent hours examining her patient caseload. Personality disorders, clinical depression, addictions, obsessions, inability to set limits, phobias, eating disorders. You name it, she dealt with it. But not one of her patients had dangerous psychotic tendencies. She and the detective would have to direct their energies in other areas.

Other areas, but definitely not the ones they'd fallen into this morning. She'd agonized half the day over what had happened. One minute they were talking, and the next she was in his arms. The memory sent traitorous trembles dancing along her nerve endings.

The events of the last two days had battered her defenses and left her emotions raw and exposed. Fear and anxiety stalked her every step. It was only natural she'd desire strong arms about her. Only natural she'd crave personal contact. And how much more personal could you get than a kiss?

She touched her lips, outlining them with her fingertips, reliving the sensation of Jack's mouth on hers. She closed her eyes and forced her mind to control her thoughts.

The feelings churning inside her were reactions to stress. The same thing might well have happened no matter who the investigating cop had been. This had nothing to do with Jack Carter.

Someone with less psychological knowledge might fall into the trap of situational attraction, but not Susan McKnight. If she ever got seriously involved, it would be a sensible relationship with a man who held the same interests as her, the same values, the same basic personality type. They would bond slowly and completely, not be pulled together by some animal need born of fright and immediacy. She would not give in to it again.

*7:00 p.m.*

THE AFTERNOON HAD brought rolling claps of thunder, jagged cracks of lightning and a downpour that flooded the below-sea-level streets of New Orleans. It hadn't brought Jack Carter. He'd called to say he was detained by an emergency. Susan fumed. What bigger emergency could you have than a serial killer on the loose who could strike again at any moment?

She arranged the last dirty dish in the dishwasher and poured in the detergent as the doorbell rang. Her breath caught. Don't let it be another message, she prayed silently. Not from *him.*

The bell rang again.

"Somebody's here," Rebecca called, running from her bedroom, two steps ahead of her brother. "I hope it's Detective Santa."

"I'll get it, Rebecca." Susan hurried to the door, stopping to peek through the peephole. At first all she saw was fir needles. Then a head appeared around the green mass.

Jack, of course, standing next to an evergreen that dwarfed even him. Her first inclination was to leave the door locked. But a dead bolt and a couple of inches of solid wood would not deter *Detective Santa.*

She eased the door open, and he barged in, dragging his tree behind him.

"Wow!" Rebecca squealed, jumping up and down.

Timmy joined in the chorus, echoing his sister's "Wow" and then starting his own chant. "A Christmas tree! A Christmas tree." He yanked on the leg of Susan's pants to make sure she saw the monstrosity.

Jack stood the fir against the wall. "Ho, ho, ho. Merry Christmas," he said, reaching down to pick up Timmy and swing him into the air over his head before depositing him back on the foyer floor. Timmy squealed and laughed all the louder.

Susan lost the attempt to control her temper. "What is the meaning of this, Detective Carter?"

"Detective Carter?" He faked a pout. "What happened to Jack?"

"Just answer the question. Why have you brought a tree to my apartment?"

He scratched the five-o'clock shadow that dotted his chin. "It's Christmas. You didn't have one. You and the kids need some holiday spirit. My cousin runs a Christmas tree lot, and I got it cheap. Take your pick, or all of the above."

She didn't laugh at his poorly timed humor. Undaunted, he flashed his boyish smile and resumed his conversation with the kids.

"What do you think, Beck and Tim? Is it big enough?"

"Pick me up so I can touch the top," Timmy begged. Jack lifted him to his shoulders.

"It's wonderful," Rebecca crooned, running her fingers over the needles, as tenderly as if they'd been chiseled from gold. "Wait until I tell Missy Sippen. She said their tree is six feet tall, but this one must be twenty feet."

"Nope, only nine, but that's way taller than Missy Sippen's," Jack assured her. He stepped past Susan and peered into the living room. "So where do you usually put your tree? I'll set it up for you. No charge."

"How thoughtful." Fortunately, her sarcasm flew over the heads of the kids. Unfortunately, it didn't appear to faze Jack.

"If we pulled that green chair out from the wall, it would fit in that corner. But if you have a better place..."

"I've never had a tree in this apartment."

"First Christmas in a new place. That's always fun."

"I've lived here for three years. I don't decorate for Christmas."

"Really?" Jack stared at her as if she'd just confessed to burning the American flag. "I'm sorry if I overstepped my bounds. Is it a religion thing?"

"No, it's not an issue of religion. I usually celebrate the day quietly with friends."

"Quietly? I tried that once when I was twelve and had chicken pox. It was a real bummer."

"Can we decorate it tonight? Pleeeeese, Auntie Mom." Rebecca danced around the tree.

"We don't have any ornaments."

"We can make some. We made all our decorations

for the tree at school. The first-graders made the chain. I'm real good at that, and I have red and green paper in my school bag. You could give us some of your glue.''

"We could string popcorn," Jack said, coaxing. "And I can make super bells and stars out of aluminum foil."

"Oh, let's do it!" Rebecca sang.

Jack shot a pleading look in Susan's direction. "Christmas trees mean a lot to kids."

One look at the children's faces, and Susan's resistance drowned in a sea of guilt. She should have been the one thinking of Rebecca and Timmy, not some man who barely knew them. She should have realized how much something as simple as a tree would mean to them. She hadn't. The truth was, buying a tree had not even occurred to her. Not in the midst of a murder spree. So why had it occurred to an admittedly hard-edged cop?

"If Auntie Mom can come up with a pair of scissors, we're in business," Jack said, his eyes locking with hers and apparently reading her acquiescence.

"Okay. I can provide the scissors, but I'll need some help popping the corn."

The kids exploded in excitement. Jack squeezed her hand. Warmth flushed her skin. Situational attraction, she reminded herself. All the same, the effects were almost overpowering. As the song said, she had better watch out.

"I'm a master popcorn popper," Jack boasted, following her into the kitchen while Rebecca and Timmy raced away in search of colored paper.

"Somehow I knew you would be."

"I hope you're not angry, about the tree, I mean."

"You should have asked me first."

"I know. That's a bad habit of mine. I'm an impulsive kind of guy."

"I'm not an impulsive kind of woman."

"So I've noticed. But maybe you should be. All work and no play makes for boring memories."

She poured a smattering of vegetable oil into a pot. "My memories are adequate."

Jack leaned against the counter, watching her. "Adequate. That must make for some great late-night fantasies."

She turned and met his gaze. His dark eyes taunted her, and a new tingle of anticipation crawled up her spine. She fought the feeling.

Jack Carter had no right to barge into her private life, no right to make friends with her young charges. No right to be in her kitchen, popping corn, making ornaments, making fun of her life-style. No right to remind her that she was a woman with urges that hadn't been satisfied in a very long time.

He was a cop and she was his link to a murderer. No matter that he blamed his impulsiveness for his actions. She seriously doubted he did anything without a reason.

"Exactly how does this evening fit into your crime investigation, Detective Carter? Is getting close and personal supposed to make me more amenable to revealing personal secrets of my patients?"

"The thought crossed my mind. I gave it up immediately. I don't think anyone makes you do anything you don't want to, Drag—Dr. McKnight. My reasons for bringing the tree over are purely selfish."

At least he admitted it. She added some popcorn to the oil.

"I'm a long way from home," Jack continued. "And seeing as how we have a dangerous murderer on a holiday rampage, it looks like I won't be flying out to Abilene this Christmas."

"I'm sorry." She was. Sorry that Jack wouldn't be going home for Christmas and sorrier that he got to her so easily, made her react inappropriately to everything he did. "It's hard for me to think about Christmas trees knowing someone might be murdered any second."

"I know. I spent the afternoon questioning Maggie Henderson's family, searching for a link between her and you. Nothing seemed to click, but I'll let you look at my findings tonight and see if anything jumps out at you."

The corn started popping, and Jack shook the pan with a ferocity more suitable to fighting off street criminals. Susan had misjudged him again. He'd obviously spent the day working on leads. Now he was thinking of Rebecca and Timmy.

"This is enough for the kids to start on," he said, pouring the popped corn into the pottery bowl she'd set on the table. "Unless they eat more than they string." He sprinkled salt on the popcorn and then held up a bite for her to sample. She parted her lips and he slid the fluffy nugget between them and onto her tongue.

"Perfect. You have a way with popcorn as well as children."

"Experience. I was the oldest of nine children. Mom and Dad both worked in the family business, so we all took a share of the household chores. Mine was usually cooking and babysitting."

"I'm surprised you didn't marry and have a houseful of kids of your own." An unexpected tightness settled in her chest. "Or, are you married?"

"Not now. I tried it once, a few years ago. It didn't work out. Fortunately, my wife found out she didn't like living with a cop before she got pregnant. But I have a passel of nephews and nieces back in Texas. Uncle suits me better anyway. No dirty diapers, no homework, no discipline.''

''All fun and games.'' Her counseling tendencies took over. ''I'd say you might be shortchanging yourself. Just because your first marriage didn't work out doesn't mean you couldn't be a good husband and father.''

He stepped closer, his eyes flashing, his smile devastating. ''Dr. McKnight, are you proposing to me?''

''No, of course not, I...'' Susan's face burned, and she was sure it glowed a bright hue of crimson. Damn him. She wasn't used to being flustered. She picked up the bowl of popcorn and headed for the living room to decorate a Christmas tree with Jack Carter.

No doubt about it. She'd taken complete leave of her senses.

IT WAS TWO HOURS, four bowls of popcorn and a dozen renditions of ''Rudolph the Red Nosed Reindeer'' later when Susan tucked Rebecca and Timmy into their beds and settled into her chair. She took a sip from the goblet of wine Jack had waiting for her.

She hated to admit it, but the evening had been fun. A striking contrast to the way her day had started. But now the holiday merriment was over and she and Jack were returning to a world of terror. The rapid swing between the two extremes set her stomach churning.

''I have the printout here on all the patients who were at the Center during the year you worked there.'' He handed her the computerized list. ''The names with asterisks by them are still there. The others have been released, moved to a prison system or transferred to another facility. This is the code I used to designate which.'' He tapped the end of his pen on the legend for his codes.

"How do you do it, Jack? You play as if you don't have a care in the world and then jump back into your cop role like it was your life."

"It is my life. All of it. The good, the bad and the ugly. There were three murders in the city last night, two the night before. That brings the count to seven for the week, and we still have tonight to go. I face this kind of violence day after day, year after year."

"I don't see how you survive."

"I couldn't do anything else. It's in my blood, the same way being a psychologist is in yours. But enjoying life's in my blood, too, and I don't make apologies for it. It keeps me sane."

"And out of psychologists' offices."

"So far."

Susan went through the list. She'd been at the Center for one year, six years ago. She'd done an internship with her father and then realized that working together brought her no closer to him than just being his daughter had. He cared far more about work than any human being. She'd left then and pursued her own career.

The list of names she was looking at now was just that. Except for a few patients she'd been genuinely fond of or seriously disliked, the names on the list didn't jell with faces or facts. Six years and hundreds of patients later, it was impossible to remember accurately.

Frustration took over her reasoning. "I can't do this, Jack. I can't look at a list of names from the past and decide one of these people is a serial killer today. I know what you want, but I just can't pick one out and say, okay, this is the man. Go get him and all of this will be over."

"I'm not asking you to. All I want are possibilities, leads. A place to start. So far we're hitting dead ends."

"There's Gabriel."

"I'm working on that. I need something to place him at the scene of the crime or else find a link between him and Maggie before I can bring him in for questioning. But, believe me, I haven't ruled him out. I'm having him tailed tonight. I'll know if he comes near here."

"What if we're looking in the wrong places? What if the killer's not one of my patients and never has been or if there's some link not connected with my role as psychologist? That's possible, isn't it?"

"Anything's possible." He took her hand and gingerly pulled her to the couch beside him. "Let's consider other options. Have you ever received threats?"

"No."

"Has anyone been stalking you?"

Susan took a deep breath. "I'm not sure."

Jack sat up straight, his eyes penetrating steel. "Either you've been stalked or you haven't. Which is it?"

"Lately, I have the feeling someone's watching me."

"Since the murder, you mean?"

"No, before that. The first time was about a month ago. I was leaving my office later than usual. The streets were deserted, except for a few passing automobiles, but it was as if I could feel someone watching me."

"What did you do?"

"I looked around. I didn't see anyone so I dismissed it as a case of nerves."

"Was that the only time?"

She sighed. Feelings without facts to back them up. The detective was going to write her off as a paranoid fruitcake. Still, she plunged ahead. "One evening, the kids and I came home from the park about dusk. When we walked in the door, I noticed a funny smell."

"Define funny."

"Actually, not so much funny as different. It was woodsy, acrid, like someone drenched in a bottle of aftershave. So strong it was nauseating. Similar to the odor on the note the other night, but much stronger."

"So you think someone had been in your house while you were out? Someone wearing an overdose of cologne?" His eyebrows arched questioningly.

"At first I did. But the alarm was still set."

"Did you call the police?"

"And tell them I smelled a strange odor in my French Quarter apartment? They'd still be laughing."

Jack flexed his hands into tight fists and then straightened them, over and over, like some bizarre ritual. Finally, he turned and took her hands in his. "You have to be careful, Susan. All the time. There's no way to know what this man will do next."

Susan swallowed the fear that balled in her throat. She had to stay rational, work with Jack, outplay the lunatic at his own game. She could never do that if fear paralyzed her mind.

"I don't want this man near the children, Jack. I'll pay for extra protection if I need to, but I want them guarded at all times. And I don't want them to know what's going on. They've come so far this year, made unbelievable adjustments. I won't let a madman steal their happiness and security away."

"It's not just the children I'm worried about." Jack's voice was low and husky. "*You* have to be careful, Susan. Of everybody. Sometimes the very people you trust the most are the ones who turn against you."

Something in his voice set off new alarms inside her. "You sound as if you have someone specific in mind." She thought about the people in her life whom she trusted the most. One name popped to the front of her mental list. "You surely don't mean Lucy. She can barely kill spiders. They're part of God's plan."

"I'm talking about your secretary, Bobby Chambers."

Susan stiffened in protest. Jack was way off base. "Bobby's not a psychopathic killer. He's a hardworking guy who's trying to get ahead in life. He goes to night school two nights a week. He's studying to be a computer programmer. Once you meet him, you'll know the idea of his being a murderer is preposterous."

"I have met him."

"When?"

"In your office last night. He was at your desk, reading files."

Anger swelled instantly inside her, until she thought she might explode. As always, she maintained control, forcing her voice to remain steady and firm. "What were you doing in my office last night, Detective Carter?"

She listened while Jack detailed events from the night before. If he was telling the whole truth, she would fire Bobby immediately. What he had done was extremely unethical, but he wasn't a killer. If she was that wrong about Bobby, she might as well take down her sign and find a new profession.

"Why didn't you tell me about this sooner?" she demanded.

"It slipped my mind this morning."

"It didn't suit your purpose this morning."

"You're right." He walked to the piano stool and sat, fingering the keys. Finally, he turned to face her. "I have a personality problem. You probably already recognize the signs. I get too involved in my work. When a young woman gets strangled, I take it personally."

He got up and paced the room, his hands fisting as the muscles in his arms grew taut. "When I know there's a madman walking free on the streets, especially one already planning the murder of his next victim, I don't eat, I don't sleep, and I don't play by the rules. I can't, because the killer doesn't.''

He turned to face her, his eyes dark and penetrating. ''But I will find this man, Susan. And I will stop him. If that makes me a monster, then I'm a monster.''

She stood and faced him. Her words struggled past a lump in her throat. ''And kissing me and decorating a tree with my children are all a part of doing whatever you have to in order to find your man?''

''No.''

He captured her gaze, and she felt the tension crackle between them. She stood her ground and didn't back away.

''Rebecca and Timmy are wonderful children,'' he said, his eyes boring into hers, their smoldering depths eating away at her resolve. ''I enjoy every minute I spend with them. You should learn to do that yourself.'' He stepped closer. ''But when I kiss a woman, it's because I find her desirable, because I damn well can't stop myself.''

His hands fastened on her shoulders. His face was inches from hers. Unwelcome desire rose inside her. The same smoky desire she read in Jack's eyes. She tilted her face toward his. And then his lips were on hers, demanding, devouring. She swayed against him, stunned by the power of his kiss and the emotions boiling inside her.

The inhibitions that ruled her life went up in smoke. She wanted Jack's mouth on hers, his tongue tangling with hers, his arms pulling her ever closer, exactly the way he was doing right now.

When Jack finally pulled away, she struggled for balance and for the reasoning power that had vanished with Jack's kiss. "We shouldn't..."

Jack stopped her in mid-sentence. "Don't analyze what just happened between us, Susan. You wanted it. I wanted it. Let it go at that. We have enough to fight without fighting each other."

She stepped away from him.

"Don't worry. I have to go now. The beeper at my waist is going crazy. I'll talk to you in the morning. In the meantime, don't leave this house unless you talk to me first. Do you understand?"

"I'm not a prisoner."

"No, but if you mess with me, you will be. I will not let you get killed just because you're too stubborn to listen to reason. Now lock the door behind me."

Before she could respond, he was gone. Her breath came in shallow gasps, and she leaned against the heavy wood door frame, too shaken to move.

Long minutes later, she went to the bedroom and stripped. She needed a shower and sleep. She needed her brain to work and her body to respond to her own dictates and not the sensuous advances of a man who was temporary and all wrong for her.

Situational attraction, born of proximity and the bonds of necessity. How many times had she told patients to ignore the fiery emotions such encounters generated? How many times had she been amazed at their inability to do so, even when the attachment it produced brought them nothing but pain?

She took a deep breath and stepped into the shower. She'd deal with this tomorrow. Tonight, she needed rest.

*Sunday, December 19*
*1:30 a.m.*

SHERRY HORNSBY SAT upright in the bed in her new townhouse, the one she'd moved into when she'd left Gabriel. She shivered in the dark, listening. The house was quiet. She must have dreamed the noise that woke her.

No, there it was again. A tearing and scraping sound. Fear pummeled her insides. "Gabriel, is that you?" No one answered her call, but a cold draft stung her skin. Someone had opened a window or a door. She grabbed the phone and frantically punched in 911. The phone never rang. The line was dead.

"Gabriel, if that's you, say something, or I'll shoot." Only she was lying. She had no gun. She looked around for anything that would do for a weapon. Opening the drawer by her bed, she rummaged for something sharp. Nothing was there but a metal nail file. She clasped it like a knife.

There were shuffling sounds outside her bedroom door now. She jumped out of her bed just as the door to her bedroom swung open.

"Don't hurt me, please don't hurt me." She tried to run from the masked and cloaked figure, but strong arms wrapped around her. She fought, biting and scratching wildly with the metal file. But she was no match for the intruder's strength.

The man bound her arms and legs and then threw her across the bed.

"I'll do whatever you want. Just don't hurt me," she begged as the silk scarf grew tighter around her neck. "No, please..." Her words died in her mouth. She tried to breathe as pain shot through her lungs and the room turned black.

# Chapter Six

Lucy Carmichael stirred in her bed. An eerie feeling of contentment spread through her body, like someone had snuggled up beside her. She stretched to get a better look at the clock. It was hours past the witching hour, but she felt totally bewitched.

"Is that you, Stephen? Were you missing me like I miss you, or do you need to tell me something?"

There were no answers to her questions. She didn't expect there to be. It had been almost a year since her husband had suffered a heart attack and died, but nights like this she felt him just the same, and she liked the feeling that he was watching over her.

Not that she was afraid of staying alone. She'd spent the biggest part of most nights alone even before Stephen had died. Musicians kept lousy hours, and Stephen had been one of the best horn blowers in New Orleans. But back then she'd known he'd be coming in when the night's work was done. Knew he'd be there in the morning, sleeping soundly next to her, his big, hairy arms wrapped around her ample breasts.

She sighed and huddled under the covers. Life had to go on. That was what Dr. McKnight said. Fortunately, the doctor had done more than talk. She'd recruited Lucy's help, and that had been the one blessing the year had brought.

Tending Rebecca and Timmy during the day had turned her life around, given her a reason to wake up in the morning. Now the days rushed by, the way days were meant to do. But the nights were still the pits.

Except when John came around. He'd never replace Stephen, but he took her to dinner occasionally, and he made her laugh. Best of all, he never pushed for affection she couldn't give him. He accepted the truth. She'd been Stephen Carmichael's woman for twenty-five wonderful years, and that was enough happiness for any woman.

And that was exactly what Susan McKnight needed, a man like her Stephen had been. Bigger than life, as cuddly as a teddy bear but tough as a Louisiana alligator when he had to be. It would take a man like that to get Susan to loosen up and let herself fall in love.

The wind picked up, whistling and groaning its way around the corners of the French Quarter apartment. Lucy pulled the covers tighter around her and closed her eyes, hoping sleep would return. It didn't. And counting sheep had never worked. That left warm milk or reading. Just to be on the safe side, she'd try both.

Throwing her legs over the side of the bed, she wiggled her toes into a pair of tattered slippers and turned on the lamp. The kitchen was downstairs and to the rear of her roomy apartment. It was bright and airy by day, opening onto the sheltered courtyard, but by night it was dark and cold. One hand following the wooden railing, she made her way down the stairs, not stopping until she stood in front of the back window.

She stood quietly, staring into the shadows of a moonless night. The only light came from the background of a city that never slept. Leaves tumbled in the wind, and water from the fountain sprayed a fine mist over an azalea that had no more sense than to bloom in December.

Something moved in the shadows, a figure low in the bushes. Too big to be a cat or a dog. Why, it looked like a person. Lucy went to the door and eased out into the brisk air to get a better view. It was a person, near Rebecca's window. The figure rose to standing position. It was someone tall, a man, with some kind of dark cloak over him.

Lucy stepped back inside and grabbed the phone. Fingers flying, she punched in 911 and gave them the address, her voice shaking so that she could hardly speak.

But the police might be forever in getting there, and someone was breaking into Susan's apartment. Someone would hurt those precious children. She bent over, reaching into a bottom cabinet and pulled out a heavy iron skillet.

"Help me, Stephen," she whispered, easing out the back door again. She took a few steps. "Get away from that window!" Her scream carried easily across the courtyard. The man turned. For a minute, she thought he would come after her. But he didn't. Instead, he threw something at Susan's back door and took off running. He went up and over the brick wall holding on to a rope of some kind that disappeared when he did.

Lucy ran across the courtyard, banging on the back door just as the lights came on in Susan's upstairs bedroom. Lucy waited in the cool night air. When a policeman in uniform opened the door, she cast a grateful look to the sky. "Thanks, Stephen," she whispered.

"Who are you?" the policeman asked.

"The woman who called you. You certainly got here fast." She stooped and picked up the white envelope from the walkway by Susan's back door.

Susan squeezed past the cop and took Lucy's hand, pulling her inside. "What happened, Lucy? I woke up to your banging on the back door and a policeman ringing the front doorbell."

Lucy told her about the man at Rebecca's window and then handed her the envelope. That's when she knew something serious was going on. The color drained from Susan's face as she ripped open the envelope and pulled out a folded sheet of paper.

Susan read the note and then dropped it to the counter as if it might burn her fingers. "Get Detective Jack Carter," she said to the policeman. "Now!"

*9:00 a.m.*

"WELL, LOOK WHAT the cat dragged in. What brings you to the precinct of stale coffee and fresh murders this time of the morning?" Casanova rolled into Jack's cubicle, the morning newspaper under one arm and a cup of coffee in his hand.

"Business. The McKnight killer struck again. At least he claims that he has. We haven't found a body yet."

"Another note?"

"Yeah. He's consistent, if nothing else."

"Serial killers usually are. At least he's not including souvenirs yet. Do you have the note?"

Jack picked up a piece of paper from his desk. "The

original's being checked for prints. I copied the message.''

Casanova read the note out loud. ''Dear Dr. McKnight, I hope you're enjoying your surprises. You'll find the next one soon, I'm sure, or at least one of your patients will. She was a lovely woman and strong. She put up quite a fight. You would have been proud of her. Until next time, Happy Holidays.''

Casanova dropped the paper onto Jack's desk. ''The man's a real charmer. How did he deliver this one?''

''Walked up to a downstairs window at Susan's apartment and cut the screen. He'd planned to make a house call. Fortunately, Susan's babysitter, who happens to live across the courtyard, woke up and saw him. She called 911.''

''How did that happen? You have a guy posted there.''

''There were actually two cops there at the time, but they were in the front of her place. You can't see the back side of the apartment unless you're inside the courtyard. You can get there through the covered parking area if you have a key or you can come through a side gate the same way.''

''Don't tell me this creep has a key.''

''No, he came over the brick wall off the side street. He used a rope that he'd anchored to a No Parking sign. He left the rope so we could see how ingenious he was.''

''Fingerprints?''

''They're still checking.''

''So what's next on the agenda?''

''These computer printouts.'' Jack picked up the stack and let them fall back to his desk. ''Every unsolved murder case involving a young woman for the last five years. The name of every known murderer in the city who's free to prowl the streets because some judge decided jail was not criminal-friendly.''

''So you're checking out the city's naughty, not nice. That has to be a long list. Any new developments?''

''Yeah. But not from that list. I also had a guy checking out Bobby Chambers.''

''I thought he didn't have a record.''

''He doesn't, but he does have a gambling problem to the tune of about $20,000 and his creditors are the you-no-pay-we-breaka-your-leg type.''

''But how would killing young women help him?''

''I don't know. Maybe he's working off his debt by taking care of someone's hit list. In that case, the notes could be a plan to send us off on a wild goose chase and keep us away from him.''

''That's pretty strong stuff. Do you think Chambers is the killer type?''

''That's one of the unanswered questions. I'm not sure he's involved in any of this, but I know he's not perched on the pedestal Susan thinks he is. I want him tailed.'' Jack picked up a dart and hurled it at a dart board on the back wall. It landed a few centimeters off dead center.

''You're losing your touch,'' Casanova said. He reached into his shirt pocket and pulled out a jade-handled dart, the one he'd won as state darts champion a couple of years ago. He took careful aim and let it fly. ''Bull's-eye,'' he said. ''Some of us just have it.''

''So you better enjoy it. That's the only thing you can beat me at.''

''Yeah, yeah, dream on, good buddy.'' Casanova dropped into a chair. ''Did you have Gabriel tailed last night?''

"I tried. He's apparently disappeared, at least temporarily."

"So the real questions are still unanswered. Who is the killer and how is he choosing his victims?"

Jack drew a big question mark on a sheet of paper and then punctured it with an angry jab of his pencil. "And when does our psycho get around to his victim he's had in mind from the beginning?"

"The dragon lady?"

Jack nodded, his gut wrenching at the thought.

"How is she handling all of this?"

"Unbelievably well up to this point, although the last note has her really shaken. She doesn't know about her secretary's gambling problems, yet."

"At least, not from you. He may have hit her up for money if he's that desperate."

"Maybe, but I don't think so. She trusts him *implicitly*."

"So, what's next?"

"The Chief is on his way over for a briefing. I want more men, lots more, and I need them now. He's just going to have to pull them off of other assignments. And I want complete protection for Susan and the children. Every second of the day."

"I'd be careful on this one, Jack."

"I'm not afraid of the Chief. He's always backed me when I'm right, *eventually*. And I'm always right."

"Yeah, and modest. But I wasn't talking about the Chief. It's the killer you'd best be careful of. A man like that won't hesitate to take out anyone who's in his way."

"That's exactly why I'm taking matters into my own hands. I don't want another body on my conscience."

"Then you'd better move fast. You know I'm here if you need anything."

"Yeah, then how about taking care of this for me?" Jack presented him with the task of tracking down every man who'd been at the Potter-McKnight Center when Susan was there and who wasn't there now.

"I can handle it."

"Good, now I'll go tackle the Chief." And after that he'd have to pay another visit to Susan. This morning's note had pulled her patients back into the equation whether she wanted them there or not. She could give the records freely or he'd take her to court. Lives depended on fast action. Hers included.

He grabbed his jacket from the back of a chair. Someone walked into the main office whistling "Jingle Bells," and Jack picked up a wad of paper and hurled it at the sound. His favorite time of the year had suddenly turned sour on him.

*11:00 a.m.*

JACK STOPPED a minute to talk to the police officer who was reading the newspaper in Susan's front office, before barging in. Susan was all but buried behind a stack of sky-high files on her desk.

"Do you work twenty-four hours a day?" he asked, straddling a chair on the other side of her desk.

"I couldn't sleep. I've been here in my office since right after you left this morning, going through these files and trying to find some connection between the notes and my patients."

"Have you uncovered anything?"

"Nothing."

Her voice dropped in disappointment, and Jack stared

at her across the desk. Dark circles surrounded her eyes. He considered reaching across the desk and taking her hands in his. He'd like to ease her fears, promise her everything would be all right.

But Susan McKnight wouldn't be convinced by empty assurances. And he couldn't protect her or anyone else if he let emotion rule his brain. So, he might as well get down to the dirty business at hand. "I know how you feel about confidentiality," he said, bracing himself for her argument. "But I have to be able to look at your files. Time may be running out on our next victim."

"I agree." She tapped her pen on an open manila folder at her fingertips.

"What do you say we get started?" he said, standing and walking around the desk to get a better look at the file she had open in front of her."

"Pull up a chair, and I'll show you what I have. I've pulled the charts on all my married female patients that even remotely mesh with the clue about valuing relationships. I've developed a hierarchy based on potential." She moved over to make room for the chair he'd retrieved from the other side of the room.

Jack picked up the nameless file on top of the stack. He opened the file and perused the contents. All identifying information had been blacked out. His pulse jumped sky-high on a new wave of agitation.

"I'm sure you didn't ruin your original files, Susan. That must mean you spent hours and packs of paper copying everything so that you could make them sterile enough for me to examine."

"I've given you the information you need."

"No, you've given me the information you *think* I need. That's not necessarily one and the same."

"I have to protect my patients."

The frustration of the last few days built up inside him like a dam ready to burst. Last night she'd kissed him as though she never wanted to stop. Today she treated him like a two-bit voyeur.

"Why did you go to all of this trouble, Susan? Do you really think I give a damn what your rich clients do with their own time? Do you think I care who they sleep with or what they do behind closed doors in fancy hotels? I'm trying to stop a raving lunatic from wrapping a cheap silk scarf around some innocent woman's neck and pulling until she can no longer struggle for that last breath of oxygen." He stood and shoved his fists into his pocket.

"I didn't mean to offend you, Jack."

"You didn't." He paced the room. "I'm too thick-skinned to be offended by psychological *indelicacies*. I'm just weary of fighting the good people and the bad people. You, the Chief, the press."

"I'm not fighting you, Jack. I'm just doing what I have to do. I thought you understood that. Do you think you're the only one who's upset by this?" Susan's voice was shaking, but her chin jutted out defiantly. "The man was at Rebecca's window last night, a few feet from her bed. Don't you know that I would do anything I can to stop him?"

Regret balled in Jack's gut. It wasn't enough that Susan had to deal with a lunatic who filled her life with terror; it wasn't enough that she was working day and night to stop the man before he killed again. Now she had to deal with accusing tirades from the cop who was sworn to protect her.

"I'm sorry, Susan. I was out of line." He touched her hand.

She pulled away. "No need to be sorry. You said what

you were thinking. The events of the past few days have us both on edge. We can't trust *any* of our emotions at a time like this."

The phone on her desk rang. She put her hand on the receiver but didn't pick it up. On the fourth ring, the answering machine started to hum and a shaky male voice filled the room.

"Dr. McKnight, this is Gabriel Hornsby. I need to see you at once."

Susan yanked the receiver from the cradle. "Don't hang up, Gabriel. I'm here."

Jack punched the button that let him listen on the other phone.

"It's Sherry, Dr. McKnight."

"What about her?"

"I was right about her all along. She finally told me that she was in love with someone else. She was never coming back to me."

"People sometime say things they don't mean."

"Not Sherry. She always said exactly what she meant. She just didn't value relationships like you told me I had to do."

Susan struggled for breath as Gabriel's words rolled through her brain. The same words as in the note. "Where are you, Gabriel?"

"I'm here, in Sherry's town house."

"Is Sherry there?"

"Yes, but you can't talk to her. No one can."

"I'm coming over there, Gabriel." The phone went quiet. "Gabriel, are you there?"

"I'm here." His voice broke into a shuddering sobs.

"Tell me Sherry's address. I'm coming over to be with you." She kept her voice calm in spite of the dread that knotted inside her. She scribbled down the number and street.

"Hurry, Dr. McKnight. I need you."

"Don't go anywhere. I'm on my way."

## Chapter Seven

Susan was only a step behind Jack as he rushed up the walk to Sherry Hornsby's new town house. He'd ordered her to stay at her office when he'd dashed out the door.

She'd ignored him, and she hadn't caught her breath since. Not even in the car, when he'd swerved through traffic at breakneck speed, the portable siren and blue emergency light in his unmarked car attacking the Sunday drivers with a shrill vengeance.

A woman was dead, and one of Susan's patients would find her. Was Sherry victim number two? Had Gabriel killed her? Susan's mind reeled with the frightening possibilities.

Jack banged on the door. It flew open almost immediately, and Gabriel stood just inside. His hair was scattered in wild disarray, and blood drizzled down the side of his face from a jagged scratch across his forehead. Susan's gaze went from him to Jack's hand, which was resting on the handle of his gun.

She tried to push between them, but Jack held her back.

"Where's your wife?"

"You don't want to see her."

Jack yanked open the screen door. "Step aside, Dr. Hornsby. We're coming in."

"What happened to your forehead?" she asked.

Gabriel wiped his hand across the wound. "I don't know." He stood stolidly, as if in a trance.

Susan left him to follow behind Jack as he walked into the living room. "Sherry!" Susan called her name, but there was no answer.

Fear engulfed her, catching her breath and sending blood rushing to her head. She watched and listened as Jack searched the living room and kitchen, opening and slamming doors, looking for some sign of Sherry, or her body.

When he found nothing, he headed for the second floor, taking the stairs two at a time. Jack opened the door at the head of the step and pushed inside. Susan stepped in right behind him.

The bed was made with a flowered coverlet and Sherry lay beneath the covers, her head resting on a lace-edged pillow. She was still, but not sleeping. One arm hung off the side of the bed, lifeless. And her face…

Susan turned away at the sight and leaned against the door. That's when she noticed Gabriel, standing behind her, a wrinkled silk scarf in his hand.

"Why don't you tell us what happened, Dr. Hornsby?" Jack's voice was smooth and reassuring.

Susan stared at him, amazed at yet another facet of the impulsive detective. She knew that in the fragile state Gabriel was in, yelling or treating him roughly would only send him further into his shell, but she hadn't expected Jack to key in on that.

He stepped closer to Gabriel. "Was this scarf used to strangle Sherry?"

"Yes."

Gabriel handed the multicolored square to Jack. The silk fabric unfolded as the scarf changed hands, releasing the same nauseating scent Susan had detected on the notes. She stepped away, moving to the staircase and clutching the banister for support.

"Sherry's dead," Gabriel said in the same monotone he'd used since they'd arrived. "I'll miss her, but she won't sleep with other men anymore." He wiped a hand across his eyes as a tear escaped. "I only wanted her to love me."

"I'm going to have to take you with me, Gabriel. You'll need to answer some questions." Jack read him his rights while Gabriel stared off into space.

"He can't be questioned in this condition," Susan said. "He needs to be hospitalized."

"Then he'll be held in a facility where he can get help until he can talk."

"He's my patient. I want a say in where he's held."

"You'll have to take that up with the judge. I'm the lowly detective who digs up the evidence and makes the arrest. After that, it's out of my hands."

Jack took the handcuffs from his waist and snapped one bracelet around Gabriel and the other around the banister at the top of the staircase. Gabriel made no move to stop him or to protest.

Susan walked silently out the door and into the brisk December air while Jack called in the crime team. Suddenly, she was consumed with an ache for all the potential for happiness Gabriel and Sherry had lost.

And Jack's words echoed through her mind. Fun, laughter, children, the little things. Those were the keys to making the world right, to overcoming the bad that surrounded them. Right now she desperately needed a taste of those little things.

As if in answer, a Christmas carol wafted on the air, no doubt carried from a neighbor's stereo. The chorus rang out, loud and clear, promising peace on earth, good will toward men. Tears burned in Susan's eyes and she closed them, blotting everything from her mind except a Christmas tree with popcorn and shiny foil ornaments.

And two wide-eyed children singing "Silent Night."

*5:00 p.m.*

SUSAN SIGNED her name to the last Christmas card and sealed it before adding it to the stack. The morning's events still weighed heavily on her mind, but she'd done all she could for Gabriel. She'd talked to the judge and he'd placed him under hospital arrest. The staff psychiatrist had assured her he was getting the best of care.

She hadn't seen Jack since he'd had a policeman escort her home. Her part in the case was nearly over, but she was sure he was busy collecting evidence. She had no doubt he'd tie up the case successfully. In spite of her early misconceptions, he was a competent and dedicated cop. The nightmare could finally come to an end.

She was sorry for Gabriel. Sorry for Sherry. And deeply regretful that in spite of months of therapy, she had not been able to help Gabriel or to see this coming. Her father had told her years ago she didn't have the psychological makeup for dealing with criminally aggressive psychotics.

She'd taken it as a putdown then. Maybe he'd only been telling her the truth. She'd certainly failed Gabriel.

"Auntie Mom, will you be mad at me if I tell you that I believe Santa Claus is real?" Susan turned to find Rebecca perched on the ottoman by her slippered feet.

"Of course, I won't be mad at you. I can't dictate your beliefs to you."

"What does dictate mean?"

"To dictate means to force someone to do, or believe, what you say."

Rebecca stood and leaned over the arm of Susan's chair. "That's good. I don't want to disappoint you or anything, but I asked Santa for something very special, and if I don't believe in him, I won't get it."

Susan wrapped an arm around Rebecca's tiny waist. "Why don't you tell me what you want? Maybe I could put in a good word for you."

"I can't tell. Besides, I think you're only teasing me."

"Why would you think that?"

"Because I know you don't believe in Santa, and I don't think you'd ask him for anything. And even if you did, it wouldn't help because you don't believe."

Once again, Susan was amazed by Rebecca's reasoning processes. The only problem was she had no idea how an impossibility like Santa fit into her logical equations. But then she wasn't six years old.

"How about a hot chocolate and Christmas cookie break?" she said. "We can eat dinner a little later tonight since there's no school tomorrow."

"Me too," Timmy said, jumping up from his toy cars and the road he'd built out of plastic blocks. "I want two cookies and marsh'ellows in my chocolate."

Both children followed Susan to the kitchen, eager to help. Rebecca took three cups from the counter and put them on the table, and Timmy put two marshmallows in everyone's cup except his. "I need three marsh'ellows," he said.

"Three marshmallows and two cookies," Susan said. "You must be hungry."

"I'm hungry as a bear." He made a face and growling noises to prove his point.

Susan pretended to be frightened and Timmy broke into toddler giggles that filled the room. She reached down and gave him a hug, a spontaneous one that surprised even her. He rewarded her with a sloppy kiss. Warmth tickled her senses.

A year ago, she'd never met Timmy or Rebecca. She'd only seen pictures and heard glowing reports about them from their mother. They were a lot like Carrie. She had been so full of life, so exuberant.

And she had taken the quiet Susan McKnight under her wing in college, forced her to meet people, to date, to go to parties. Forced Susan to have fun, whether she wanted to or not.

Now that Susan thought about it, her best friend, Carrie, had been a lot like Jack Carter. Perhaps that explained the crazy bond she felt with him. She probably wouldn't have to worry about that problem anymore. She might never see him again.

She swallowed the unexpected lump in her throat and ignored the emptiness that lay heavy in her heart. She might miss the arrogant, sexy detective, but it was for the best. Intimacy had never come easily for her. Neither had openness or flexibility. And they were all trademarks of the gregarious Jack Carter.

Situational attraction. That's what they'd experienced. And now that the situation was over, the attraction would die. The two of them would never mesh.

"Auntie Mom, do you think Detective Carter could be the real Santa Claus?"

Susan stopped stirring the chocolate. She had to answer this question with care. Believing in Santa was one thing. Believing in Jack Carter was another entirely.

"Detective Carter is a policeman, Rebecca. He just puts on a Santa Claus suit for fun, but that doesn't make him Santa Claus."

"But he doesn't dress like a policeman. He dresses like Santa Claus, at least sometimes he does. And he laughs like Santa."

"Anyone can say ho, ho, ho."

"Not like he does. He shakes when he laughs, just like it says in the book, but he's not fat. I think he went on a diet since they wrote that story about him."

"'The Night before Christmas' was written many years before Jack was born, Rebecca. It isn't about him."

"Maybe. But you just never know about Santa Claus. That's what Missy Sippen says."

Susan poured the warm chocolate into the mugs and sat at the table with the children. "I say we talk about something besides Santa and Missy Sippen. Let's talk about—"

"I know," Rebecca broke in. "Let's talk about angels. Miss Lucy says her husband used to be a horn blower, but now he's an angel. He just sits around in the clouds blowing his horn and watching out for her."

Susan choked on the sip of chocolate that had just started down her throat. "Why don't we talk about cats?" she said, desperately seeking a topic she knew something about. "I've been thinking we need a cat around here."

"We can't get a cat," Timmy said, sticking his finger into the chocolate and dunking his marshmallows so that he could watch them bob up again. "I already asked Santa for a puppy."

A puppy. Now that was news. She had no idea Timmy wanted a puppy. The doorbell rang and Susan breathed a sigh of relief as she hurried to the door. Once again she should have known better.

Jack Carter was on her step and a holly-garlanded horse-drawn carriage was parked in the tow-away zone in front of her apartment.

She opened the door and Jack bowed low, his bright red Santa hat in hand. "I'm here to escort the lovely Dr. McKnight and her two charming charges to Jackson Square for a night of caroling by candlelight."

Rebecca skipped into the room, Timmy right behind her, a half-eaten cookie squeezed in his hand, dropping crumbs every step of the way. He was the first to spot the horses.

"Wow! Horses! Can we ride in the sleigh?"

"It's a carriage, not a sleigh, but if Auntie Mom says it's all right, you can ride in it all the way to Jackson Square."

Rebecca pushed through the door and stood on the stoop. "Oh, boy. White horses. Wait until I tell Missy Sippen about this."

"So what do you say, Auntie Mom? Is it a go?" Jack shot her the familiar persuasive look, his smile devastating, his eyes twinkling mischievously.

A hundred reasons why it shouldn't be a "go" ran through Susan's head. But how could she say no to Rebecca and Timmy now that they'd seen the horses? Still, she glared at Jack. "You promised no more surprises."

"I did?"

"You did."

"I can't imagine why. I love surprises. It's going to be the perfect night. Clear as a bell and the temperature's still in the sixties. If we leave now we'll have time to walk around a bit, then grab a quick bite and still make it back to the square before the caroling starts at seven."

"While you were making all those plans you might have called and asked me if I wanted to go."

"No, I couldn't have." He placed his lips close to her ear, his breath fanning her cheek. "If I had, you would have said no, and I can't deal with disappointment, not on the Sunday before Christmas."

"So can we go, Auntie Mom, pleeeease?" Rebecca dropped to her knees and pleaded, her big eyes directed upward. Susan had no idea where she'd learned that maneuver.

"Pleeeeease," Timmy squealed, trying to climb on Rebecca's back while she was down. She knocked him off and he fell to the floor laughing.

"Okay." She didn't get a chance to say more. Both kids squealed their delight and went tearing off to get their sweaters.

"Don't forget to potty," Jack called after them. "The French Quarter's short on bathrooms."

Susan opened the hall closet and pulled out a gray cardigan. Jack held it for her while she slid her arms inside. His hands rested on her shoulders, his right thumb tangling with a curl that had escaped her topknot. Susan's skin prickled, and the crazy tingle his touch always produced started again. This time it danced up and down her nerve endings like a firefly in a windstorm.

"I'm glad you agreed to go," he said, turning her around to face him.

"Why? Is this another of your attempts to combat missing your family at Christmas?"

"No." He leaned closer. "It was an unabashed attempt to see *you* again."

The room grew warm, and Susan struggled for breath and for control. *Situational attraction.* She made a mantra of the words, determined to keep everything in its proper perspective. The only problem was her pounding heart did not appear to be heeding her warning.

*6:45 p.m.*

INSIDE THE WROUGHT iron gates, Jackson Square had been transformed into a glittering sea of holiday-bedecked carolers and candlelight. People from all over the surrounding area had made their annual trek into the city to celebrate the season by joining in the citizens' choir that numbered in the thousands.

"When does the singing start?" Rebecca asked, as soon as they'd made it through the gates.

"When the archbishop arrives," Susan explained. "When six o'clock mass is over, he'll lead a procession from Saint Louis Cathedral onto the stage they have set up in the center of the square. That signals the official beginning of the caroling."

"Will that be a long time from now?"

"About ten minutes," Jack answered. "Can you wait that long?"

"If I have to." She looked at her song sheet and picked out the words she could read. Timmy made a plane out of his, flying it up and down and in between Jack and Susan.

"Look, Auntie Mom. There's Lucy."

"It certainly is."

"Are you by yourself tonight?" Jack asked, after the initial greetings. "If you are, we could use another caroler."

"I was supposed to meet my friend John in front of La Madeline's, but he never showed up. I guess he got held up somewhere or else I missed him in the crowd."

"Go find Mr. John. He might be lost," Timmy countered, with the unarguable logic of a three-year-old.

Lucy patted him on the head. "If I run into him, I'll tell him you were looking for him," she said. "But I don't think he'll get so lost he can't find his way home."

Rebecca took Lucy's hand. "We came in a carriage pulled by white horses. Just like Cinderella at the ball."

"You did!" Lucy looked duly impressed.

"Detective Santa brought them."

"Is that right? Well, if I see John I'll tell him what he missed. If he'd been here on time, he might have seen you climb down from your chariot."

"We would like to meet him if he shows up," Susan said. "We've heard so much about him."

"We already met him," Rebecca boasted.

"Really, when was that?"

"He's been by the house a couple of times when I was sitting with the children," Lucy explained. "I hope you don't mind. He was only there a minute or two each time. I didn't let it keep me from watching the children."

"I'm sure you didn't," Susan consoled. "I just didn't realize he'd been there. Anyway, I would like to meet him just because he's a friend of yours."

"I'll tell him that. He'll be delighted. He's always asking questions about you. I think he's impressed I work for Doctor Susan McKnight."

"I doubt that he'd ever heard of me before he met you."

"Oh, no. He'd heard of you, all right. He perked right up and got interested as soon as I mentioned your name the first time."

Susan talked a few minutes with Lucy before Lucy dragged Jack into a discussion about recent changes in the New Orleans Police Department. Then Lucy saw someone else she knew and hurried off to chat some more.

"A nice woman," Jack said.

"Because she agreed with you about the changes?"

"No. It's her eyes. They're clear and trusting. And she looks right at you when she talks. People with something to hide always look away when they're talking to a police officer, even one out of uniform."

"Always a cop," she said.

He snaked an arm around her and pulled her close. "Not always."

Susan trembled, fighting urges too strong to ignore. She tilted her head upward, and he touched his lips to hers, feather-soft and quick, but her pulse soared.

Situational attraction. It sounded great in theory. Her mind understood it. So why didn't her body? Especially now that the situation was gearing down for closure.

The bells of the cathedral rang, and the crowds pushed in tighter. Jack reached down and picked up Timmy, hoisting him to his shoulders for a bird's-eye view as the procession led by altar boys in white robes and the archbishop made its way through the waiting carolers and into Jackson Square.

Minutes later, the singing began. Susan sang all the verses of "Silent Night," her soprano blending with Jack's deep baritone. And when Jack reached over and took her hand for "White Christmas," she didn't pull away.

The night was beautiful, lit by flickering candles, stars and the glow from multicolored Christmas lights on the balconies of the Pontalba Apartments—balconies that had stood vigil over the square since 1850.

For the first time in days, Susan let the tight cords of

worry slip from her mind. Maybe they really would have a merry Christmas.

"So who wants ice cream?" Jack offered, when the last song was over and they'd followed the crowd out of the park and into the street in front of the cathedral. He wasn't hungry, but that never stopped him from eating ice cream. Besides, he was in no hurry for the evening to end.

Rebecca and Timmy jumped up and down, voicing their approval loudly. And this time Susan gave in without a fight.

Jack took Rebecca's hand. "We have to walk two blocks to get it."

"Can I ride your shoulder?" Timmy asked, tugging on Jack's pant leg.

Jack swooped him up in his arms. He'd grown attached to the little tyke. Rebecca, too. He knew they gave Susan fits at times, but they were good kids. He'd miss them, now that the case was hopefully over and done with, at least as far as Susan was concerned. Maybe that was why he'd sprung the money for the ride to the park tonight, made his invitation so appealing Susan couldn't say no.

He looked down at Susan, watched the sway of her hips as she walked, the loose curls bouncing around her neck, the way she tilted her head just so when she talked to Rebecca. No. It wasn't the kids that had brought him around tonight.

He started across the street, but Susan tugged at his elbow. "Let's walk down Royal Street. I love looking in the shops this time of the year. The displays look so tempting."

"Surely you've done your Christmas shopping by now," he teased.

"Bought, wrapped and hidden away. I don't buy many, and I never wait until the last minute. I hate impulse buying."

"Me, too. I always start my shopping a full twenty-four hours before Christmas, most years anyway."

Rebecca yanked on his hand, pulling him to a stop in front of a shop window. "Isn't she beautiful?" she crooned, pointing to a porcelain doll in a miniature high chair.

"She is beautiful, and she has freckles on her nose, just like you." He touched a finger to the tip of Rebecca's nose, and she giggled softly.

Susan stood back to scrutinize the doll. "Is that what you want Santa to bring you for Christmas?"

"No, ma'am. Not this year. I've already asked for something else." She squeezed Jack's hand conspiratorially. "I only want one thing for Christmas, and I hope Santa brings it to me. Do you think he will, Detective Santa?"

Jack thought for a minute and then wished he had the ability to kick himself in the seat of the pants. He'd completely forgotten about Rebecca's request on the night she'd met him. She wanted a husband for her Auntie Mom.

He'd been too busy making sure her Auntie Mom stayed alive to even think about that again. Now that he had, he didn't like the idea at all.

Susan going for ice cream with some other man, decorating a Christmas tree with someone else, crawling into bed beside some stranger who didn't know how to make her laugh. He groaned inwardly at the thought.

"Sometimes Santa can't deliver what you ask for, Rebecca. When that happens, he brings something else just as good, maybe better.''

"I don't want anything else.''

"Not even a beautiful doll with freckles?'' Susan coaxed.

"No, ma'am. If I can't have what I asked for, I guess I don't want anything.'' She left the window and started walking.

Regret balled in Jack's gut as he followed along. He should have never played along with Rebecca, let her believe even for a few minutes that he might be the real Santa. Now she had her heart set on something he couldn't possibly deliver.

Hell, he didn't even know anyone good enough for a woman like Susan to marry. And if he did, he wouldn't introduce them. He was a good loser, but not that good.

This time it was Susan who stopped. "I know the woman who owns this shop,'' she said. "She travels to Europe twice a year to buy antiques. Like that table in the corner with the inlaid design. It must be worth a fortune.''

"Another of your well-heeled patients.''

"Proof that money does not buy happiness. Carolina is always searching for something more. Her workaholic husband doesn't help matters.''

"I want ice cream,'' Timmy said, taking Susan's hand and tugging. She followed his lead, but she was still quiet when they rounded the corner and entered the ice-cream shop. Worrying about Carolina Taylor, Jack suspected.

Her file had been one of the two Chambers had out the night he'd found him doing his after-hours snooping. He didn't remember anything particularly unusual about her except that she liked to have fun and her husband didn't accommodate her.

Rebecca and Timmy looked at everything before deciding on double dips of chocolate. Jack chose a sundae, loaded with hot fudge sauce and whipped cream. Susan had a dish of vanilla.

Rebecca and Timmy took their cones to the back counter to watch the movements of an animated Christmas display. Jack pulled up two chairs and pushed them to a nearby table where he and Susan could keep an eye on them.

Susan toyed with her treat, barely tasting it.

"You're wasting good ice cream."

"I know. I was thinking about Gabriel."

"It's always hard to accept that someone you know could take a life." He took her hands in his. Tonight might be the last chance he ever got to hold them. The last time he sat across from her, her knee brushing his.

He hadn't felt this way about a woman in a long time. The last time he had, the ending hadn't been happy. There was no reason to think another marriage would be any different, but it wasn't marriage he was considering. Just a relationship, for however long it lasted.

He captured her gaze. Her eyes reached out to him, and he knew he couldn't just walk away without at least giving them a chance. And he might never have a better opportunity than tonight.

# Chapter Eight

Jack thumbed through Susan's stack of CDs while she tucked Rebecca and Timmy into bed. He chose a jazz instrumental he'd heard Susan play before and inserted it in the player, adjusting the volume to a romantic level.

He'd told her he wanted to talk, and she'd suggested he stay while she got the kids bathed and bedded. She might not have agreed so willingly had she known what he wanted to talk about. Nonetheless, he'd joined in the fun, splashing water with Timmy and reading a story to Rebecca.

But now that the moment of truth was nearing, he wondered what in hell he was doing playing house in the residence of one of New Orleans' best-known shrinks. Lowly homicide detectives did not socialize with the likes of her. But unless he was way off base, she was feeling the same attraction he was.

Could it have only been four nights ago that he'd left here wishing he never had to face the dragon lady again? A couple of murders ago. Gabriel Hornsby, prominent New Orleans surgeon, goes over the edge and kills his wife.

The newspaper reporters and television news anchors were having a field day. He'd seen the excitement in their eyes when he'd explained the notes and the fact that Hornsby was also charged in the death of Maggie Henderson. If it was up to him, the news media would get only the barest of facts, but he wasn't the Chief. And he wasn't looking for any political favors.

Susan would draw front-page headlines. Reporters would be on her doorstep and in her face. Poor reporters. She'd send them running for cover. Even they were no match for his dragon lady. The police department would be hounded by criticism. No matter that they had solved a major case, the people would howl and demand to know why they hadn't been warned earlier that a serial killer was on the loose. The life of a cop.

"I see you found the compact discs," Susan said walking through the door.

"Is it too loud for the kids?"

"No, they're used to it. I like to listen to music at night after they're tucked in. Could I get you something, a glass of wine or coffee? I think there might even be a couple of Dixie beers in there."

"Beer sounds good, but let me get it. You've had a long day. What can I get you?"

"Since you ask, I'd love a glass of Chablis. I have some chilled."

Jack went to the kitchen. Finding the chilled wine and the beer was easy, but he had to open several cabinet doors before he located a crystal flute. Like everything about her life, Susan's cabinets were neat and organized.

The addition of two children as lively as Timmy and Rebecca must have really thrown her into a tailspin. No wonder they had her buffaloed half the time. And no wonder Rebecca thought Susan needed help handling them. Rebecca was a very astute little girl.

By the time he returned to the living room, Susan had

pulled her feet under her on the couch and tucked them beneath a quilted throw. Long tresses of sandy blond hair had broken loose from the oversized barrette on top of her head to cascade about her shoulders.

The heart he liked to think of as being as tough as nails did a flip-flop. The intimidating doctor had dropped her untouchable façade. She looked vulnerable and innocent, and so enticing it was all he could do not to gather her in his arms and carry her off. Like a caveman claiming his woman.

But she wasn't his woman. If he were half-smart, he'd just tiptoe out the door and out of her life before she threw him out. But then no one had ever accused Jack Carter of being overly smart where women were concerned.

He dimmed the light and settled down on the couch beside her, his heart suddenly beating fast. He felt like a schoolboy who was about to steal his first kiss.

She rearranged a pillow behind her back and stretched her feet back to the floor. She reached for her glass of wine and took it from him, her fingers brushing his.

An accidental touch, but it added new fuel to the fire that was burning inside him. She took a slow sip, the wine wetting her heart-shaped lips.

He cautioned himself to move slowly, although slow was not his style. But rushing wouldn't work with Susan. He settled back against the cushion, his gaze fastened on her. "The kids seemed to have a good time tonight. They have a way of livening up the season."

"I never dreamed Christmas would mean this much to them."

He ran his hand along the back edge of the couch and traced the lines in her neck with his fingers. "So you're not still mad at me for bringing the tree?''

"No. I guess I owe you an apology for my tirade."

"An apology sounds nice. But I have a better idea for payment." He leaned closer, his fingers tangling in her silky hair. One hand under her chin, he tilted her face upward until their gaze met and held, and all his words of caution went up in smoke.

"What is it you want?" Her voice was throaty, breathless.

"I want to kiss you, Susan. I want you to forget all of your rules, all of your psychological jargon and kiss me back. No strings, no promises, just two people who aren't afraid to admit they have feelings for each other."

"But—"

"No buts. If there's someone else, or if I've misread the signs, all you have to do is say so. I'll walk out of your life the same way I walked in."

Susan tried to think logically, to come up with all the reasons she should get up and escort Jack to the door. He was all of the things she wasn't. Open, spontaneous, exciting. A relationship between them would mean never-ending conflict. Neither of them could give what the other needed.

Besides, she didn't have time for a man in her schedule right now. Balancing a career and tending to Rebecca and Timmy took all of her time and energy. The excuses were all there and all valid. She knew what she should do.

But her body refused to listen. Jack was beside her, the way he had been through all of this. Strong and masculine, warm and funny, and unbelievably exciting. She ached to feel his lips on hers, to press her body against his.

No strings, no promises. Just two people who wanted

and needed each other. That's what Jack said, and she'd never needed anything more.

She raised her head and touched her lips to his. And once she did there was no pulling away. The fatigue and stress she'd fought for days vanished, and all she felt was passion, as real as the arms that wrapped around her. It rose inside her and consumed her.

She swayed closer and his arms tightened around her, his fingers searing a path down her neck and along her shoulders. Her insides melted, and she opened her lips and welcomed his thrusting tongue.

Finally, it was Jack who pulled away. With a finger, he traced a path from her forehead, to the tip of her nose and down to her lips. "You're quite a woman," he whispered, his eyes devouring her, as if he had to memorize every line before he looked away.

She trembled, and he rocked her against him.

"I have to go now," he said, "before I do something you're not ready for."

She sucked in a steadying breath. In the morning, she might feel gratitude for his consideration. Tonight she longed for more. "You don't have to leave. I'll make coffee."

He stood without letting go of her hands. "No, if I stay, it's not coffee I'll be wanting."

She knew what he wanted. She wanted it, too, but she couldn't make love to him. Not yet. For her, making love couldn't be separated from commitment and involvement. It was not nearly the same as a no-strings kiss.

"Do you want me to stay, Susan?"

"Not tonight, Jack." She whispered the words through a cottony dryness that all but choked them away.

Trembling, she undraped the throw that still covered her legs and stood. "I'll walk you to the door."

She did and they said their goodbyes as he poked his arms into his jacket. "It's been quite a day," he said, turning the key in the lock.

She slid into his arms and lifted her face for one last taste of him. The kiss was full on the lips, and she held on until she had to come up for air. "I'm not usually like this," she murmured, letting go of him and leaning against the door frame.

"You don't say," he teased. "Who'd have ever guessed?"

She watched until he'd disappeared in the darkness. No telling where he'd left his car, since he'd shown up tonight in a white carriage.

No matter. He'd be safe. No mugger in their right mind would mess with Jack Carter. Even in a Santa hat, his size and swagger broadcast that he was a man to be reckoned with.

She locked the door and turned out the light. The events of the day, the sleepless night, the wine and the kisses were all taking their toll on her equilibrium. Perhaps they'd also taken their toll on her senses.

The next thing you knew she might even start believing in Santa. She'd already fallen under the spell of Detective Jack Carter, and that was far more dangerous.

She touched her fingers to her lips. They were sensitive, and swollen and still warm from his touch. It couldn't last long. Nothing this good ever had, but when it crumbled, she'd have a few good memories tucked away in her mind.

And then on cold, dark nights when the nightmares of this week came back to haunt her, she could pull them out and use them to frighten the evil away.

THE MAN MOVED in the shadows, watching as the detective left Dr. McKnight's apartment. Apparently, there was more than police business going on between the two of them. He'd guessed as much tonight at the square when he'd seen the way he looked at her.

Two people out on the town and in love. They thought they had it all behind them. They'd change their mind when the next note was delivered.

It was all amazingly easy. Crazy! He'd show the good doctor. He was still smart enough to fool her and that arrogant detective. He couldn't wait to finish what he'd started, couldn't wait to hear Susan McKnight beg for mercy.

His would be the last face she saw before she closed her eyes forever. But still that wouldn't be enough. He had to think of something more frightening than just killing her, something more terrifying than the threat of killing her patients. He had to do something that would reach inside and tear the heart right out of her.

He wanted to be around to watch on the longest day of her life. Then he could leave this all behind him.

Jack disappeared around the corner, and the lone man stepped out from the shadows. Just another man walking the streets of the French Quarter. But he had plans to make and business to take care of. Christmas was almost here.

*Monday, December 20*
*8:00 a.m.*

JACK GROANED and buried his head under his pillow. It didn't help. The phone kept up its shrill ringing. Giving up, he grabbed it and managed to bark a hoarse hello into the receiver.

"Don't tell me you were still asleep."

"Just get on with it, Casanova. And skip the sarcasm."

"You sound like you're in a bad mood. You're about to be in a worse one. Have you read the headlines?"

"No, I had been spared opening my eyes until you called."

"You'll find them interesting, and so will your dragon lady. But that's not why I called you."

"Good, I'd hate to think you just couldn't wait to ruin my day."

"I checked out the names on that list you gave me yesterday."

"A little after the fact now."

"Or maybe not. One of the men looks very interesting."

Jack untangled himself from the sheet and slung his legs over the side of the bed. "You've got my attention."

"J. J. Darby. Arrested seven years ago for strangling his girlfriend with a silk scarf. He was suspected of killing two other girls the same way, but they couldn't tie him to those."

"Possibly strangled three girls with a silk scarf. Where was that?"

"The first two were in Arkansas. The last was in Texas, but he wasn't necessarily consistent. He went home after killing his girlfriend and shot both of his parents."

"So, why was he at the Center instead of rotting in jail?"

"Some psychiatrist determined that he was incompetent to stand trial. So he went on an extended vacation to the Potter-McKnight Center."

Jack jumped to his feet and started looking for his shoes. "But he's not there now?"

"No, he attacked a nurse last year. They moved him to the state hospital and put him under maximum security. He was a model patient. Restrictions were lifted and he escaped two months ago."

Jack balanced the phone between his chin and chest while he yanked on a pair of jeans. "I still think Gabriel's our man."

"In which case you're not interested?"

"I didn't say that."

"So what did you say?"

"Put out an APB, and I'll see you in about ten minutes."

IT WAS 9:15 when Susan pulled into the parking spot in front of her office. She'd slept late this morning, the first time she'd done that in years, but five days of living with constant fear and dread had taken its toll.

Stepping out of the car, she smoothed the lines in her blue suit skirt and dodged a newly formed pothole. A neighbor in the house two doors down waved from her porch, and Susan waved back.

Everything quiet and normal. All the better for dealing with her own conflicting emotions. She'd gone to sleep last night thinking wonderful sexy thoughts about Jack Carter and playing with the idea of what it would have been like if he'd stayed.

She woke this morning thinking about him, too, but the thought patterns had changed drastically. What could she have possibly been thinking to let him kiss her like that?

No, she might as well be honest. She hadn't let him

kiss her; she'd kissed him. Over and over again. And she'd wanted more.

One minute the man was driving her up the wall, the next he was driving her crazy with desire. He made her forget everything she knew. They simply didn't mesh.

She turned her key in the lock and pushed the door open. No sign of Bobby, though he was usually at work before eight. Maybe he had an idea what awaited him when he came in. She just hoped he made it before the first patient arrived at ten.

Susan deposited her handbag on the top shelf of the wooden storage cabinet and clicked on her message machine, making careful notes of each call. Then she started the coffee and checked her appointment book, the same routine that she followed every morning.

Unlike Jack Carter, she was a creature of habit. The fewer the surprises, the more comfortable she was. Control and order were her mainstays. She took a deep breath, determined to push thoughts of Jack Carter aside.

Situational attraction. That's all it was, and it was over. She'd miss him. So would the kids, but they would all get over it. Life was full of disappointments, and learning to live with them was an important part of emotional growth.

God, it was amazing how much she sounded like her father. And how she'd hated those lectures when he'd delivered them. *Now, Susan. Life is serious. You have to learn to keep your emotions under control and don't expect too much. That way you won't be disappointed.*

And she'd believed him. She still did. She couldn't help but imagine how Jack's parents had indoctrinated him. *Now, son, life is cold, so always wear your fur-trimmed red felt hat and any time you're not working, go out and have a jolly good time.*

She smiled in spite of herself. It died on her lips when Bobby Chambers walked in the front door. She waited until he'd hung his jacket before asking him to come into her office and have a seat.

He dropped the newspaper on her desk as he did. "You and Gabriel Hornsby made the headlines this morning."

Susan picked up the paper and scanned the first few lines of text and the caption under the late Sherry Hornsby's picture. *New Orleans surgeon kills wife and one other woman in jealous rage.*

"I was shocked," Bobby said. "I knew Gabriel was having all kinds of problems but I didn't expect him to pull a stunt like that."

"Neither did I." She folded the paper and laid it back on her desk. "Exactly how did you know Gabriel was having all kinds of problems, Bobby?"

He straightened in his chair. "I just assumed he was since he comes to see you." He crossed his leg and stared at the carpet. "And the other day he called and changed his appointment because he didn't want to miss even one."

"Detective Carter tells me he found you in the office Friday night. He said you were reading patient files."

He shifted in his chair and focused on a spot just left of her head. "I stopped by and did a little work on those records you wanted databased. I'd had an argument with Linda and didn't feel like going home to an empty house. I told the detective that. I even suggested he call you that night."

"Detective Carter didn't see it exactly that way."

"Oh, he saw it that way, all right, Doctor McKnight. He just wanted an excuse to get *his* hands on your confidential files. I told him you wouldn't like it. He ignored me.''

Susan was sure the last statement was true. Not only because Bobby was finally looking her in the eye, but because she knew Jack. ''My records are confidential, Bobby. I explained that to you fully when I hired you.''

''You made it clear, and I haven't breathed a word of anything about your patients to anyone.''

''I hope you haven't. When I asked you to database the charts, I requested you put in the name, beginning and ending dates of therapy and diagnosed condition. All of that information is on page one of each individual file. There is no reason for you to read any other part of the records.''

''I understand. I really do, and I need this job. You won't catch me doing anything unethical. I was upset that night, and I may have read a little of Gabriel's before I put it away, but it won't happen again.''

''Good. You're an excellent assistant, and I'd like to keep you, but if I ever find out you are reading my files, I will fire you on the spot. Do you understand?''

''Yes, ma'am, and you don't have a thing to worry about.''

Susan dismissed him. She'd always liked Bobby, but this morning she had the feeling he was not telling her the truth. Maybe he was just nervous over the prospect of losing his job. Or maybe she was only reacting to Jack's suspicions. Either way, she'd keep her eyes and ears open. One more slip-up, and he would be immediately dismissed.

*8:00 p.m.*

SUSAN PULLED a dripping Timmy from the bath and wrapped him in an oversized fluffy towel. ''All nice and clean and ready for story time," she said, giving his wet hair a vigorous rub with the end of the towel.

"Isn't Detective Santa coming over tonight?"

"Detective Jack," she said. "Not Santa, and he isn't coming over tonight. You'll have to settle for a story from me."

"Rebecca says he's Santa."

"Rebecca is teasing you. Now, let's get your pajamas on so we can read a story."

"I wish Detective Santa was coming over. He's funny."

Susan felt exasperation all the way to her toes. Mostly because she wished Jack was coming over, too. But Gabriel was in custody, and Jack was probably already moving on to a new case and new problems.

She held Timmy's pajama bottoms while he wiggled into them. "Now over the head." Timmy closed his eyes and butted his head through the hole. "What story would you like to hear tonight?"

The doorbell rang. "It's Detective Santa," Timmy yelled.

Susan went to the door with Timmy and Rebecca trailing behind. She looked out the peephole, but no one was there. Fear consumed her, stealing her breath away. She tamped it into submission. The nightmare was over.

Gulping in a large helping of air, she opened the door.

Rebecca slipped past her. "Look, Auntie Mom, a present. Who do you think it's for?"

"I don't know. We'll have to look and see." Susan read the tag. *Dr. Susan McKnight, Holiday Greetings.*

The blood rushed from her brain. Not again. It couldn't be happening again. She'd seen Gabriel standing over Sherry's body with the murderous scarf in his hand, and he was in jail. She stumbled inside and locked the door.

"Open it, Auntie Mom," Timmy insisted.

"No." Dread grabbed at her voice, making it squeaky and weak. She forced it to steady. She couldn't upset the children. "It's not for me."

"But it has your name on it," Rebecca said.

"It does, doesn't it?" She was being ridiculous. Holiday Greetings was as common a seasonal greeting as Merry Christmas. She tore off the paper with Rebecca's and Timmy's help. Her pulse raced as she opened the box lid and peered inside.

"It's just an old envelope," Rebecca complained. "That's not a real present."

Susan walked to the phone. Fingers shaking, she dialed Jack's pager number. The terror of Christmas present had returned.

# Chapter Nine

Monday, December 20
8:45 p.m.

This time when the doorbell rang, Susan had a good idea it would be Jack. She let him in and he followed her to the kitchen. The package sat on the middle of the table, the envelope still inside and unopened.

"So this is the latest surprise?"

Susan threw up her hands in exasperation. "Gabriel is in custody. The nightmare is supposed to be over. So how do you explain this?"

"I should have warned you."

"Warned me?" Her voice rose.

Jack went back to the door and scanned the area. "Where are Rebecca and Timmy?"

"I put them to bed." She cornered him near the door. "Warned me about what?"

"Party crashers. When a story gets the kind of coverage this one did, there's always a kook or two who want to get in on the fun."

Susan paced the room. "Are you telling me this newest note is unrelated to the previous ones, that it was not sent by the same person?"

"You got it. Party crashers hope to have *their* note make the headlines tomorrow. You know, local psychologist receives another threat. The killer is still on the loose. Then the city panics, and our kook breaks an arm slapping himself on the back for creating a stir."

"I picked the right profession," she said. "This is a sick world." She picked up the envelope and handed it to Jack. "It has the same scent as the others. Open this and read the note, Jack, and then tell me it's a party."

Jack took her hands and led her to a kitchen chair, hooking another with his foot and dragging it over so that he could sit beside her.

She shook her head vigorously, trying to clear the clouds of confusion and the dread that had churned in her stomach ever since the letter had arrived. "So, you think this note is a hoax."

"It looks that way."

Susan took the envelope from Jack and held it under her nose, touching only the tip of the paper, so as not to destroy fingerprints. She was getting to be an old pro at this.

The same nauseating odor as before assaulted her senses, and the same fear bared its fangs and gnawed at her control. "You're wrong, Jack. It's from the same man who sent all the others. The odor is the same."

"Anyone can dab aftershave or men's cologne onto an envelope. The evening news shows gave all the gory details, including the fact that the envelope was scented with a man's cologne. With a little luck, our party crasher could have used the same one Gabriel did. With even less luck, he could have used one with a similar odor. There's probably a lot of women who don't find this particular fragrance offensive."

"Okay, so I have a supersensitive nose. Read the note, Jack. I've put off the inevitable long enough."

Jack opened the envelope and studied the note. " *'Holiday Greetings.'* Our first indications that this is a copy," Jack said. "He didn't start with 'Dear Dr. McKnight,' and he said Holiday Greetings instead of Happy Holidays."

"Maybe he was in a hurry. Read the rest of it."

"The newspaper reports of the murder were most entertaining, but surely you didn't believe them. I'm still here, Dr. McKnight, working on your next holiday surprise. Christmas is only a few days away."

Jack walked to the cabinet and took a plastic bag from the shelf. "I need to take this with me. There's a good chance the man who sent this has played this game before. His prints may be on file."

"So you think I should just go to sleep and not worry about this note?"

"Exactly. But to put your mind at ease, I'll have an officer reassigned to watch your house. He'll be right outside the door. Now, how about a cup of coffee?"

"No, my nerves are shot as it is."

"Maybe you should prescribe yourself a tranquilizer."

"Psychologists don't prescribe pills. We call in a psychiatrist or a family doctor if drugs are necessary. But I prefer mind over matter whenever possible. That's why I like the whole truth. You're not positive this note isn't from the killer. If you were, you wouldn't reassign a guard to my house."

Jack stared at Susan, wishing he could deny her claims. But he couldn't. The shadow of a doubt had nagged him all day. J. J. Darby had apparently dropped of the face of the earth. And J.J. liked to strangle young women with silk scarves.

He knotted his hands into fists, a useless gesture. There was nothing to bang them into. So he might as well level with Susan. She'd never buy less than the full truth. "What were your duties when you were interning at the Potter-McKnight Center?"

Susan raised an eyebrow, but she answered. "You name it. I counseled with patients, did small group-therapy sessions, handled paperwork no one else wanted to bother with, wrote grant proposals."

"Did you have enemies while you were there?"

"You always have enemies in that type of setting. But nothing I took seriously. Some patients hated me, others thought they were in love with me. Often it was the same patient at different times in the therapeutic process."

"Tell me about some of the patients that you thought hated you."

Susan rubbed her temples and tucked a few loose hairs behind her ears. "What are you getting at, Jack?"

"Before we arrested Gabriel today, I had a check run on all the men who were at the Center when you were there who aren't there now. One of the names that came up was J. J. Darby. Do you remember him?"

"No, but it's been six years since I was there. I remember a few of the men, but not many."

"Darby was arrested for strangling his girlfriend with a silk scarf. There had been similar unsolved murders in the eight-month period prior to that. They were never able to connect them to Darby. After he killed his girlfriend, he went home and shot and killed his parents."

"John Jasper Darby."

"So you do remember him."

"He was the very first person I did a competency

evaluation on. My father had to sign off on the evaluation as the psychiatrist, but I did most of the questioning. Together we determined that Darby was not competent to go to trial.'' She traced the subtle pattern in the tablecloth. ''Where is he now?''

''No one knows.''

Susan trembled. Jack took her hands in his. ''Every shred of evidence in Sherry's murder points to Gabriel, Susan. As far as the Chief is concerned, the case is ready to turn over to the district attorney.''

''But you think it may be Darby.''

''No, I think it's Gabriel. But you know me, I run these cases into the ground. I checked with the state hospital. He was a model patient. I checked with the Potter-McKnight Center, and they were less than fully cooperative. They only provided minimum information, and he was there almost six years.''

''Do you want me to call them?''

''No, not call. I'd like to talk to the staff personally and see Darby's records and charts for myself, just on the way outside chance that somehow Darby and Gabriel could be working together.''

''It's a long drive. Six hours when the weather's good. Tomorrow is supposed to be nasty.''

''I want you to go with me, Susan.''

She shook her head. ''I've done my time at the Center. I'll help in any way I can, but don't ask me to do that.'' Susan stood and backed away. ''If you think it's Darby, go after him. Talk to anyone you need to. You don't need me to interview hospital staff.''

''I need you to interpret the records. It's your area of expertise. All of your graduate study dealt with that population.''

''As always, you did your homework well. But don't

ask me to do this. I need to be here with the children, with my patients. I only thought I'd finished my Christmas shopping. I still have a doll and a puppy to buy. I absolutely can't drive with you to the Center.''

Jack walked over and took her in his arms. ''I need your help, Susan. We'll have police protection for Lucy and the children every second of the day. Not only outside, but sitting in the apartment if that would make you feel better.''

''No, Jack, I absolutely cannot do this.''

''We'll leave first thing in the morning,'' he said. ''You'll need to pack a bag just in case we get stuck in the bad weather and can't get back. They're predicting an ice storm for the northern border of the state.'' Jack cradled her to him.

''I really don't want to do this,'' she said, laying her head on his shoulder.

''I know.'' He touched his lips to the top of her head. ''But we'll both feel better if we're absolutely positive that everyone involved in Maggie's and Sherry's murders are in jail.''

*Tuesday, December 21*

THE EARLY MORNING departure Jack had promised was delayed by emergencies relating to Gabriel's arrest, and it was eleven o'clock before they finally made it out of the city. Jack made small talk about pleasant, impersonal topics on the long drive up Interstate 49. Susan knew he was trying to ease her mind about leaving the children and trying to keep her from thinking about unnerving possibilities.

It worked occasionally, times when his easy laughter filled the car, times when she was reminded how it felt when he had taken her in his arms. How she had come alive at his touch.

Away from him, she could think with some semblance of reason, know that falling for Jack Carter was the worst mistake she could make. But with only a few inches separating them, she knew that it was too late to stop what had already happened. Situational attraction or not, she'd never felt this way about any man.

But if Jack was feeling the same thing, he hid it well. He was friendly but professional, a cop with a job to do. All the more reason why she had to protect her heart. When this was over he could walk right out of her life and never return. And if she let herself fall in love with him, she'd be left to pick up the pieces.

Love. She knew so little about it. And what she knew scared her to death. She closed her eyes, a futile attempt to forget the man who sat beside her, his dark hair, thick and unruly, his facial features, rugged and strong. But it was more than how he looked. It was who he was.

A man who lived life to the fullest, who wasn't afraid to play as hard as he worked. Who wasn't afraid to feel. A man who made her feel more alive than she ever had before.

But finally, stress and fatigue took its toll and she fell into a state of half sleep where she was barely aware of Jack's voice singing along to music from a country radio station. It was miles down the road before she woke up enough to realize that the sky had turned into layers of gray on gray and a light sleet was falling.

At five minutes after five, they pulled into the parking lot of the Potter-McKnight Mental Health and Research Center. Susan shuddered as old memories rose like smoke to fill every crevice of her mind. The memories weren't all bad, but none of them were especially good.

No laughter and very little warmth. It was just life as she'd known it.

She looked around, and was surprised at how much things had remained the same since she'd walked away six years ago. Walked away from her father and a legend she could never live up to, walked away from a life that made her feel inadequate and unfulfilled.

"The parking lot looks pretty empty," Jack said, as he unbuckled his seat belt and grabbed a cap from the back seat. "I'm glad I called ahead and told them we were coming or we might not have anyone to talk to but the skeleton crew and the inmates."

"The *guests*. They call them guests here, not inmates."

"Yeah, I forgot. This is the criminal version of Club Med."

"Always a cop," she said. A gust of wind caught the door and nearly blew it closed before she could get out. She pulled her coat tight and kept her head down as she started toward the manned gate. If nothing else the weather should make the interview move swiftly.

The roads were already slippery and treacherous. They'd get worse as darkness dragged the temperature well below the freezing mark. The staff would be anxious to give Jack the information he wanted and get home.

"This is a pretty impressive place," Jack commented, taking her elbow as they sloshed across the lot.

"I guess it is. I practically grew up here, so I never really thought of it that way."

"A mental hospital seems a strange place to grow up."

"I didn't actually live here, but my father was here more than he was home. I visited often."

The guard at the gate called for an escort to see them into the building. Another led them through the wide foyer and activity room and into the office of Dr. Malachi Caulder, the current administrative director. The man was short and wiry, with thinning hair, receding hairline and glasses that slid down his nose.

Jack shook the bony hand he offered and wasted no time in getting down to business. "I have a list of questions, Dr. Caulder. I'll need someone who knows the patients well enough to answer them. I'm not sure who that would be."

"I can assure you that I am familiar with all of our guests, Detective Carter, even though I've only been at the Center for seven months. I review every record on a regular basis and have seen each of the patients in individual sessions to determine their mental and emotional status for myself."

"You don't have to sell me on your merits, doctor. I'm just here to get a few questions answered."

"I've heard wonderful things about you, Dr. Caulder," Susan added. "And we really appreciate your waiting to talk with us." She shook his hand and took the seat he held for her.

"I consider it an honor to be able to assist the daughter of Dr. Kelsey McKnight."

"Thank you. Did you know my father?"

"Not well. He died before I came here, but I met him on several occasions. He was a brilliant and dedicated man."

"Yes, he was," she agreed.

"He was an inspiration to all of us in the field. Now how can I be of service to you?"

Jack jumped into the conversation. "We're trying to

find out what we can about a former inmate of yours. J. J. Darby.''

''Mr. Darby was a *guest* of ours, but he's no longer with us. He attacked a nurse approximately a year ago. The acting administrator at that time had no choice but to move him to a new location where maximum security could be provided.''

''The acting administrator?''

''Yes, it was not easy to replace Dr. McKnight after his death. The position was filled by an acting administrator until I was hired.''

Susan listened while Jack persuaded the pompous administrator to open up and tell them the name and phone number of the nurse who'd been attacked. Jessie Bailes. Susan remembered her well. Friendly and efficient, and very good with the guests.

Jack crossed his legs and leaned back in his chair as if they were here on a social call and Dr. Caulder was an old friend. ''Did J.J. ever talk about Dr. Susan McKnight?

Caulder pushed his glasses back on his nose. ''No. Most of the guests deal pretty much in the present or the distant past, things that happened when they were growing up. Childhood patterns of acceptance and rejection have been proven to be the strongest influence on personality development.''

Jack tapped his pencil on his notebook. ''I guess that's why they say the apple doesn't usually fall too far from the tree.''

''You could put it that way.''

Susan expected Jack to follow up the doctor's comment with his speech on how he spoke fluent cop talk. He didn't. Apparently he was too intent on getting what he came after.

"I'd really like to take a look at the records you have on Darby," he said. "You know charts, files, medical records, that sort of thing."

Caulder stared at Jack over the rim of his glasses. "Do you have a warrant?"

"No, I didn't think I'd need one. After all, Dr. McKnight's father founded and ran this place for years before his death. And she's an expert in the field as well. I'm sure you can trust her to examine the records of a guest who's no longer with you."

Susan got the message loud and clear. This was why Jack had insisted she accompany him today. In this place it was the shrink, as he called her, and not the cop who had the clout.

They spent the next two hours looking at every scribbled comment and reading every progress report that had ever been written about J. J. Darby. As far as Susan could tell he'd gone up and down on the emotional scales like a seesaw at a school picnic. Her father had been his therapist for most of the years he was here, and Kelsey had tried a multitude of drugs and behavior-changing techniques. Apparently none of them had steadied the seesaw for any extended period of time.

The activity room was empty when they walked through it on the way to the door. Evidently, the guests were all at dinner in the cafeteria. The television was still on, beeping, as a severe weather warning flashed across the bottom of the screen. Travel was not advised unless absolutely necessary. And then only if drivers kept to the main roads.

The Potter-McKnight Mental Health and Research Center was thirty miles from a main road.

"There's a café of sorts down the road," Jack said, taking Susan's arm and guiding her down steps that were already glazed with ice. "I noticed it when we drove in. I'd like to stop there if it's open and grab a quick bite. We'll call Mrs. Bailes from a pay phone there, or from my car phone if the café's closed."

Susan nodded and pulled the hood of her all-weather coat higher. It was a good thirty yards from the front door of the building to the gate that led to the parking lot. On a night like this it seemed a hundred.

This time the guard stayed inside his cozy guardhouse when they approached, pressing his nose against the glass to get a good look at them before he punched in the code.

The gate swung open, and Jack all but carried Susan through it, making sure she didn't fall on the concrete that had turned into an ice-skating rink in the short time they'd been inside.

A white Christmas came early, something rare for the Deep South. But this was not the frothy white snow dreams were made of. This was the ice that glazed roads, especially bridges and overpasses, making them impassable.

The kind of night people should stay inside, huddled by a warm fire. Home with Rebecca and Timmy and a lopsided Christmas tree with homemade ornaments and strings of popcorn. And a policeman standing guard.

But in spite of everything, the trip to the Center had eased Susan's mind. An emotionally disturbed surgeon who blamed her for his present problems was a much more likely candidate to be their murderer than an unstable man she'd barely known seven years ago. Especially when they'd found that surgeon practically in the act.

But information about Darby had surfaced during Jack's investigation, and he was determined to find the man. He wouldn't stop until Darby was returned to the mental hospital or to jail. If only all cops were this dedicated, she thought, there wouldn't be any unsolved crimes.

Jack eased the car from the parking spot and out the long drive that wound through a stand of pine trees. A crack rang through the night, like a shotgun at close range. Susan looked up just in time to see a giant ice-covered limb fall to the road in front of them.

Jack dodged the branch, sliding into a skid that took them to the edge of a ditch before he could straighten the wheels and get them back on asphalt.

Susan tightened her seat belt. "That was a close call. Will it be safe to drive tonight?"

"Not if this keeps up." Jack picked up his cellular phone and punched in a number.

"Are you calling Mrs. Bailes?"

"Not yet. First I want to check with the state police up here and get a report on the condition of the roads and the location of the nearest hotel."

"I really wanted to be home when the children woke up in the morning." She squirmed while Jack asked about road conditions.

"It's that bad, huh?" Jack growled into the phone.

A heavy scowl twisted his lips, and Susan knew that she'd never be home by morning. She'd be spending the night with Jack.

# Chapter Ten

*Tuesday, December 21*
*9:00 p.m.*

Susan and Jack were batting zero by the time they pulled into the meager parking lot of the motel the state police had recommended. The café was closed, and Nurse Bailes's phone was apparently knocked out by the same storm that had dipped the temperatures into the low twenties and stranded them in the northwestern corner of the state. One of the worst on record for this date, according to the radio announcer.

"I forget what a frigid difference a few hundred miles can make," Jack said. "Now I know why I moved to South Louisiana."

"A few hundred miles and the warming effects of the Gulf of Mexico." Susan stared out the car window, eyeing the motel warily.

It was no more than a low line of adjoining rooms with an almost flat roof and doors that opened onto a walk, a line of scraggy hedges, and the parking lot. The end room, the one marked office, had a dim light glowing through a pair of flimsy curtains. The rest of the place was bathed in gloomy darkness.

"Do you think it's open?" she asked, her voice betraying her uneasiness.

"Probably. There are cars parked in front of some of the units. My guess is the electricity is out."

"There's a light on in front."

"Could be an emergency lantern. But, if there's a bed, it'll beat sleeping in the car."

Susan had her doubts, but she climbed out of the warm car when Jack did. The sleet was mixed with rain now and falling harder. She hurried as fast as the icy pavement allowed. Jack gave her a hand up the two slippery steps and held the door for her.

An overweight man in tight jeans and a plaid flannel shirt looked up as they came through the door. He pushed his way out of a wooden rocker as if it were a real struggle. "You folks picked a bad night for traveling."

"That we did," Jack said, stamping his wet feet on the doormat. "Actually, it picked us. Do you have a room available?"

The man scratched his whisker-roughened chin. "I can fix you up. Ain't got no electricity though, and don't know when it'll get turned back on. Storm knocked it out a good half hour ago. Phone's knocked out, too. We got heat, though."

"Glad to hear that. What about food? Is there a place to get a bite of something around here?" Jack asked.

"The café up the road's usually open. My son runs it, but he closed early tonight. No use to stay open without electricity. You people miss your supper, I guess."

Susan wasn't sure if it was a question or a statement.

"We did," Jack said, moving over to stand beside a gas heater.

"I can find you something around here, but it won't

be no fancy meal. The nearest restaurant's in town, a good thirty miles away. Nearest motel, too, except this one. I wouldn't advise making the trip tonight. Lots of creeks in between here and there and those country bridges are narrow and slick as a…'' He shot Susan a sheepish look. ''Well, you know they're real slippery when they get coated in ice. Had a fellow run off one last year on a night not near this bad.''

''That doesn't sound like fun,'' Jack agreed.

''Nope. He lived, but his car didn't.'' The man shuffled to a low counter in back of the narrow room. ''How'd you folks manage to get stuck out here on a night like this?''

''It's a long story.''

The man chuckled. ''Probably a good one, too. We don't get a lot of business out here this time of the year. In the summer we have our regulars, fishermen looking for a cheap place to stay. There's a public boat launch about a mile up the road. They pull some nice bream and catfish out of this end of the lake when the weather's right.''

He pulled a spiral binder from the drawer and moved it over to catch the light from the lantern. ''Then sometimes we get family members visiting up at the Mc-Knight-Potter Center. But on a night like this, we might get anybody.''

He tapped his pencil on a couple of names marked under the heading December 21. ''These guys work up at the Center. They figured if they went home, they might not make it back for the early shift tomorrow, so they just stayed here.''

''A home away from home,'' Jack said, joining in the man's small talk as if they were fishing buddies.

''Yeah, I try to make it comfortable. They were drinking beer and partying earlier, but it seems they quieted down when the electricity went out. I'll leave a room in between them and you, just in case they get loud again.''

"We'd appreciate that," Susan said. She'd also appreciate a hot shower and a clean bed. And sleep. She wasn't sure any of them would be forthcoming.

"The rooms all have two double beds." He glanced at Susan's ring finger. "Will you need one room or two?"

"One will be fine." Jack answered before she had a chance to state her option.

She started to protest. She changed her mind, though she wasn't sure what stopped her. Maybe the weather. Maybe the gory images of finding Sherry's body, or maybe just the memories of the past that the visit to the Center had evoked.

She only knew she didn't want to be alone in a strange motel room on a dark and stormy night.

At any rate, there were two beds in the room. And she could trust Jack. After all, he was the one who'd pulled away when the passion burning inside her had been so strong and hot that she might not have been able to. And he'd given no indication today that he was interested in a repeat of Sunday night's performance.

The man handed Jack the key, a flashlight, a couple of candles and a promise that he'd get the wife to rustle something up in the kitchen. And if they needed anything else, they could pay a visit to the house out back where he and the family lived. That is, if they could find it in the dark.

Jack paid the man and led the way to the room. "We may be glad the lights are out," Jack said, unlocking the door and swinging it open. "I'd say this is about a half-star resort."

"I'll settle for dry."

"And warm," Jack added. He scanned the room with the beam of his flashlight. "Actually, I've stayed in worse," he said. "Back when I was a narc doing undercover."

Maybe it was just that the light was too poor to notice the faults, but Susan was pleasantly surprised herself. The two beds were separated by a large table that held a lamp and clock and a basket of dried flowers.

A large dresser hugged the opposite wall. The mirror was slightly off-kilter, but there was a tray with individually wrapped plastic glasses.

She threw back one spread and inspected the sheets. Snowy white and clean. What more could she ask for? She followed Jack to the back to complete the inspection.

"Hurray for natural gas," he cheered, turning on the faucet in the bathroom. "I see steam. Not that I doubted we could generate some ourselves."

He turned to face her, and his eyes telegraphed a smoky desire that sent her pulse spiraling upward. She forced it to steady. Leaning in front of him, she slipped a finger under the stream of water to see for herself. "Hot water, soap and lots of clean towels. You may have to add another half star to your rating."

"First I'll have to check out the mattress. Care to join me?"

Anticipation prickled her flesh. He had been deadly serious all day. Now, stranded in the middle of nowhere, he was joking and looking at her with that gleam in his eye.

She had to think rationally, remind herself of the impossibilities of her entering a relationship with Jack. They were two very different people, caught up in a

situation that had thrown them together daily in an emo-
tion-charged atmosphere. Neither of them was bound by
another relationship, so it was only natural they would
reach out to each other, connect at some intimate level
they would have never reached under other circum-
stances.

That was the psychological theory she would have
used to explain the same feelings she was experiencing
if they had been described to her by someone else. But
she'd lived a lifetime in the last few days, and she was
falling in love with Jack Carter.

Jack stepped closer. She could feel the nearness of
him, feel his breath on the back of her neck. She turned,
and his gaze locked with hers.

She longed to step into his arms, but a lifetime of
inhibitions, a lifetime void of intimacy, held her back.

"Give me the key, Jack, and I'll get our bags from
the car before the weather worsens."

"You are independent. But a true gentleman always
carries a woman's bag into his *motel* room."

He was teasing again. She let it ride. It was safer than
touching the topic of sleeping in the same room. She
busied herself, pulling down the spreads on both of the
beds and lighting the candles while Gentleman Jack ven-
tured back into the cold.

Jack returned a few minutes later with bags in hand
and his cellular phone at his ear. His conversation jarred
her back to reality. He was reporting their whereabouts
to someone at police headquarters in New Orleans, and
barking instructions as to how he wanted the search for
J. J. Darby conducted.

He swung her bag to the top of the luggage rack and
his smaller one onto the dresser. "Glad we packed
these," he said, hanging up the phone and tossing it to

the bed. "Otherwise I'd be without a razor and as hairy as our host by morning."

"You could never look like that."

"Why, thank you, Doc. I take that as a compliment, though the way you pulled away from me a few minutes ago, I would have thought you found me extremely unattractive. I was feeling downright bad about myself."

Not a chance, she decided. Self-confidence oozed from every pore of his masculine body. Better to change the subject. "I'd like to call the house, Jack, and check on Rebecca and Timmy."

"Sure. I think you should, but they're fine."

"How can you be certain?"

"I just talked to Betty Hammonds. She's the officer on duty inside the house tonight."

"Good. Lucy will be more comfortable with a woman around."

"Yeah. Hammonds is competent and genuinely nice. She and Lucy will hit it off fine. They have my cell phone number and I told Hammonds to call if anything changes."

"Then there were no new notes today?"

"Not a hint of trouble. I also talked to one of the guys who patrolled the area during the early shift. He reported that the afternoon was as smooth as the skin on a…part of the female anatomy."

"Only he said it in cop talk, of course."

"Right. I translated that one for you."

She laughed in spite of herself and realized how good it felt. The day had been far too tense, but just knowing that no more notes had been delivered and no more bodies discovered relieved some of the pressure. It looked as if Gabriel really was her tormentor, and Darby was someone else's headache.

"I'd have been translating cop talk all day if I'd known it would put a smile on your face," Jack said, sitting on the edge of the bed and giving it a trial bounce.

"No, you wouldn't. You were far too caught up in your investigation to smile yourself."

"True. But we've done all we can do for now. And tomorrow we'll talk to Jessie Bailes. She might be the one to give me a good lead on Darby. I'd like to arrest him, too. That way I could finish all this off and stamp Closed on the case file. In big, black letters."

"And start off again on a brand-new case."

"That's about the size of it."

She stared at him in amazement. "So you ride a roller coaster every day of your life. Up and down, Santa suits to dead bodies, new leads to dead ends. Don't you ever get dizzy and want to climb off?"

"Lots of times, but if I did, I'd miss the excitement. What about you, Susan? Don't you ever want to climb aboard, soar to the top, experience everything life has to offer?" He pulled her to the bed beside him.

She shuddered and sucked in a deep breath. This was no longer casual conversation, but a gauntlet he'd hurled at her feet. She had only the truth to answer his challenge. "I'm afraid I wouldn't be able to deal with the fall when I plummeted to the bottom."

He pulled her into his arms. Before she could open her mouth, his was pressed against it, hard and demanding. One fierce thrust of her palm against his chest, and the reason she was fighting deserted her.

She quit resisting and returned his kisses, pressing her body into his, exploring his back with clutching fingers.

Jack deepened the kiss, as they fell backward onto the bed. His fingers tangled in her hair; his tongue demanded and tangoed with hers. Desire rocketed through her, so intense she gasped for breath.

Jack pulled away and sat up. "I hope you change your mind about climbing aboard, Susan. If you don't, you'll miss out on one hell of a ride."

She closed her eyes but jerked them open when a loud knock sounded at the door. Jack opened it, and the man from the front desk stepped inside holding a tray.

"The little woman fixed you a plate of leftovers. It ain't the Ritz, but you won't starve."

Jack peeked under the waxed paper covering. "Fried chicken! And don't tell me that's homemade coconut pie."

The man beamed. "Yep. The little woman is the best cook this side of the Mississippi. Folks come to my son's café from all over just to get a slice of her pie. That's real whipped cream, too. Just taste it."

Jack stuck a finger into the fluffy topping, slid it between his lips and then smacked appreciatively. "It's real, all right. You tell your wife she made two starving people very happy tonight."

"I'll do that. Now I'll get out of here and let you folks eat."

Jack thanked him again, and the man finally backed out of the door. Susan pushed the burning candle back to make a spot on the bedside table for the laden tray.

"How about this for a picnic?" Jack said. "Chicken, potato salad, pickles and pie."

"And no ants," Susan added, suddenly famished. "All we need is a bottle of wine."

"Then you are in luck." Jack unzipped the duffel he'd stashed on top of the dresser and pulled out a bottle of red wine. "Merlot, 1995. A very good year."

"A wine connoisseur cop. I am impressed."

"No, I just know what I like. And I've never met a year I didn't like." He reached back into the duffel and retrieved a wad of tissue that encased a couple of wine goblets.

"And a Boy Scout, too. Always prepared."

"Everything down to the corkscrew. It's the only way to travel when you're with a beautiful woman. Actually, I visualized our stopping to toast our good fortune under the moonlight, but candlelight in a seedy motel adds a certain flair."

"It's not so seedy."

"It *ain't* the Ritz."

This time they both laughed, and Susan felt a layer of fatigue fade away. Jack did make a valid point. No matter how serious the problems, depression and worry didn't solve them. They only robbed you of the energy you needed to wake up the next morning and go at them again.

Actually, she'd often counseled patients to ease up on their worries, but she had to admire the way Jack did it—with such style.

He poured the wine and handed one goblet to Susan. "I propose a toast."

She lifted her glass.

"To roller coasters, long may they soar."

He clinked his glass with hers, and the now familiar tingle skittered along her nerve endings, creating erogenous zones of every part of her body. "To roller coasters," she echoed. And to the good sense to hold on tight and grab all the gusto she could if she ever had the courage to climb aboard.

Jack took a long sip and then set his glass on the table. "We have on far too many clothes for a picnic in bed," Jack announced. He started unbuttoning his shirt.

"Are you going to put on your pajamas now?"

"No."

She breathed easier.

"I don't own any pajamas."

The breathing grew difficult. "But what do you sleep in?"

"The raw."

The image that danced through her head sent a wall of heat roaring through her. She was sure she was blushing shamelessly and that Jack was reveling in her embarrassment.

"But since it's a special occasion, I'll leave my boxers on, unless of course you want me in the raw?"

"No, boxers will be fine."

"Aren't you going to change, Susan? I mean, that suit and the blouse with the high-buttoned collar look terrific on you, but surely you don't sleep in that."

"We're not sleeping, we're eating."

"In bed. Besides, the candles will burn out soon, and it would be much easier undressing now than in the pitch dark."

"We have a flashlight."

"Whose batteries are very weak. But suit yourself." Jack yanked his arms from his shirtsleeves and threw the unwanted clothing to the chair behind him.

Susan sat mesmerized by the mat of dark, curly hairs that carpeted his chest, by the broad shoulders and muscular frame as it narrowed to his firm waist. By his hands as they loosed his belt buckle and unzipped his jeans.

The jeans slid to the floor, and her gaze fell with them, only to climb back up his body slowly. Strong, muscular calves, punctuated with dark, stubby hairs, reminding her how long it had been since she'd been with a nearly naked man.

The knees weren't great, but they weren't bad. But the thighs were to die for, hard and firm. She imagined them wrapping around her. She swallowed and lifted her gaze a little higher.

To boxer shorts, bright green ones, with crawfish in red hats pulling Santas in sleighs. She snickered and Jack's eyebrows rose.

"Are you making fun of my shorts, lady? I'll have you know they were designed by one of the most fashionable elves at the North Pole."

"You do take Christmas to heart, don't you? Not to mention other parts of your body." She was smiling now, not only outwardly, but deep inside, in the recesses where happiness seldom reached. The warmth touched the cold edges of the fear and terror she had lived with for the past few days.

It didn't dissolve them, but it did remind her that life was too precious to waste. And it made a roller-coaster ride seem so appealing she didn't dare sit on the sidelines and watch her car leave without her.

"I'll tell you what, Detective Jack Carter, I don't think I could eat with a man dressed in as poor taste as you are right now."

"Oh, is that so, Dr. McKnight? Then what do you suggest?"

She wiggled out of her suit jacket and slipped out of her sensible pumps. Hands on her hips, she sashayed across the room, stopping close enough to bury her face in the dark hairs that cushioned his chest. Pulse racing, she let her fingers stroll the taut muscles of his stomach and then slip beneath the elastic of his wonderful Christmas underwear.

She tilted her head to face him. "I'll go for the raw,

if you will." Her voice caught on the emotion that consumed her, her words escaping in a throaty whisper.

Jack didn't wait for a second invitation. For all he knew he might be dreaming, but he wasn't waiting to see if he woke up. He swept the beautiful, untouchable dragon lady up in his arms and carried her to the bed.

"This is the first thing that has to go," he whispered, pulling the amber clasp from her hair. He ran his fingers through the silky tresses, watching in awe as her long hair spread like burnished gold across the white sheets.

She touched her lips to his chest, nibbling and kissing, and he fought the urges that threatened to steal the moment from him, make him climax long before he had tasted every inch of Susan. Before he had driven her wild with desire, the way she had him ever since their first kiss.

He captured her lips with his while he fumbled with the uncooperative buttons of her blouse. Finally the fabric parted, and he kissed his way down her neck, to the soft rise of her breasts. Soft moans of pleasure tore from her lips, and Jack ached with his need of her.

She turned on her side, and he reached behind her, unsnapping the lacy scrap of bra and pulling it loose so that her breasts spilled out. Beautiful mounds of ivory flesh, the nipples pink and puckered, as if made for his lips.

He circled one with his mouth, letting his tongue explore while his fingers moved down her taut stomach to loosen the clasp of her skirt. He wanted her undressed fully, wanted her to know pure abandonment and pleasure, wanted her to soar with him when he finally fit himself inside her.

"Tell me what feels good," he whispered. "Anything you want, just tell me."

"You, Jack. You feel good."

"I do now. If I'd slept in this room tonight without having you, I'd have gone out of my mind."

"Then you would have really needed my services."

"No more than I do now, my beautiful, sexy shrink. No more than I do now."

Together, they maneuvered themselves out of the rest of their clothing. Jack explored and caressed the exquisite curves and crevices of Susan's body, finding out what made her shudder in pleasure, what made her raise her hips and press them toward him, what made her legs open for him.

When he could wait no longer, he lifted himself over her and she guided him inside her. She was ready, so hot and moist, he thought he'd explode at first touch. He held his breath and then released it in a moan of delicious pleasure as he thrust a few more times, just enough to take her rocketing with him to the top.

Energy and emotion spent, he rolled to his side and pulled her with him. He cradled her in his arms, her fragrant hair spilling over his shoulder and chest, her body still warm, glowing in the light of the candle.

"Was it what you expected?" he asked, his mouth nuzzled in her hair.

"Oh, yes. It was wonderful. Can we do it again?"

He groaned and wondered where his next burst of energy would come from. The dragon lady had vanished. He had created another kind of monster.

*9:30 p.m.*

THE PHONE RANG. Lucy looked from the ringing instrument to the plainclothes policewoman who sat at the kitchen table thumbing through a Christmas catalog. "Should I get it?"

"Yes, just follow the instructions I gave you earlier if it's a stranger."

"To the letter." Lucy grabbed the phone. "Hello."

"Is this the sexy Lucy Carmichael speaking?"

Her pulse raced for a second before she recognized the voice. "Oh, John, it's you."

"You sound disappointed. Who were you expecting, Mel Gibson?"

"Sure, he calls every night about this time." But to tell the truth, she was just a little disappointed. Baby-sitting with a police guard for company was the most exciting thing that had happened to her in a long time. If she'd actually gotten to talk to someone dangerous, now that would really top it off. Of course, she didn't know where the danger was supposed to come from now that Gabriel Hornsby had been arrested.

"How did you know I'd be here?" she asked, when John didn't volunteer the information.

"You weren't at home, and I knew you better not be out carousing with some other man."

"I would if one had asked me," she teased, "especially since you never showed up at the caroling Sunday night."

"I got tied up. I thought I might come over for a while tonight, though. I'll bring pizza. Are you going to be at the doctor's long?"

"All night."

"Really? Is it a special occasion or is the doctor busy with a little hanky-panky?"

"Neither. She's out of town with that..." Lucy noticed the woman cop glaring at her, and she broke off in mid-sentence. She wasn't supposed to tell anyone what was going on and here she was about to blab to John.

"She's out of town on business and not sure if she'll be back late tonight or tomorrow."

"The kids must be in bed by now. I could come over and keep you company."

"You could, but I already have company. A…a friend of Dr. McKnight's is here." She sounded so secretive, she excited herself. This was almost like being involved in espionage.

Stephen was probably dying of envy. Well, not dying. But envious, all the same, that is if angels could be envious. "The friend is going to be here with me all night," she added.

"Then why does the doctor need a baby-sitter? Can't her friend handle Rebecca and Timmy when they're sleeping?"

"Not the way Lucy Carmichael can."

"Oooo, cocky little wench, aren't you? So does that mean you don't want my company?"

Lucy thought for a second. Susan had told her to go about her business as usual. And she occasionally had visitors while she was baby-sitting. Her sister had spent a whole day with them when she'd been in from Dallas, and Susan hadn't minded at all.

"You can come over for a few minutes, if you behave yourself."

"Like I had any other choice. The one time I tried to kiss you, you threw me out of the house so fast I didn't have a chance to get my coat."

"And it taught you to mind your manners. You can come over for a while, but don't be bringing me any pizza. I had a big juicy pork chop, smothered in onions, and I ate every bite."

"In that case, I'll eat my pizza first. I'll come by for a little while though. It's too cold to be roaming the Quarter on a night like this, and I'm in no mood to stay home alone."

Lucy said goodbye and hung up the phone. She'd enjoy seeing John if he actually made it over, but she'd have to be careful what she said.

Both Susan and Detective Carter had cautioned her about the necessity of keeping it a secret that a bodyguard had been assigned to the McKnight house. Lucy didn't understand it herself. It seemed awful odd to have a bodyguard when the man who'd been killing people was already in jail. But, one thing for sure, life was getting interesting.

This might not be such a bad Christmas after all.

She turned on the TV and surfed the channels until she landed on a replay of *Miracle on 34th Street*. The movie was already half over, but that didn't matter. Lucy knew it practically by heart. It was one of her favorites.

But before the movie Santa could prove his identity, the doorbell rang.

"I'll get it," she said. "I think it's a friend of mine." Officer Hammonds followed her to the door.

# Chapter Eleven

*Wednesday, December 22*
*7:50 a.m.*

Susan stretched and reached for Jack only to grab a handful of pillow. Rubbing dregs of sleep from her eyes, she sat up in bed and scanned the motel room, but there was no sign of him.

Sun streamed through the curtains, a sure sign she'd overslept. No wonder. She'd slept very little last night. Unless she'd been dreaming, they'd made love more than once, wolfing down the chicken, potato salad and every bite of the pie in between.

The gentle ache in her thighs and the odor of cold chicken bones assured her she hadn't dreamed all of it. So where was Jack now? Wherever he was, thankfully he hadn't gone there in the *raw*. His jeans and shirt were missing. His shoes as well.

Susan headed to the bathroom, stopping to retrieve her toothbrush and toothpaste and the light robe that had never been worn last night.

Last night. Warmth flooded her, as the memories rushed in. The ride on the thrill-a-minute roller coaster. She'd worried about regrets. They might come one day, but all she felt this morning was a warm and tingly sensation caressing her senses.

Tomorrow could bring anything. No, today could bring anything, but she would handle it. She always had. The difference was that now she would be handling it with the warmth of fulfillment glowing inside her.

She was gargling when the front door burst open and the chilly draft swept through the area.

"So you finally got out of bed."

"A few minutes ago. Where did you get off to?"

"To find coffee. I even have hot biscuits to go with it."

Susan poked her head around the corner. "Compliments of the *little woman,* I presume."

"The best little cook this side of the Mississippi."

"Do me a favor, Jack. Don't ever refer to me like that."

He bent down and kissed her. "Don't worry. I saw those lumpy pancakes you made Timmy the other morning."

"That's not what I meant." She swatted him with the hand towel and picked up the cup of coffee. It was hot and strong and black, the way she liked it. "What are the roads like this morning?"

"The sun is melting the ice fast, and the temperature's supposed to make it into the high thirties today. Another hour, and the roads should be clear except for icy patches over bridges."

"So now all we have to do is track down Jessie Bailes."

"Mission accomplished. The phones are back in service. She's off today, but she suggested we stop by her place. I told her we'd be there at nine."

Susan looked around for her watch, finally spying it

beneath a wadded paper napkin smeared with whipped cream. She checked the time. "Fifty-five minutes from now."

"She lives close. Apparently she has a place on the lake our buddy was telling us about last night."

"Does she know why we're coming?"

"I told her we wanted to know about J. J. Darby. She said we'd come to the right person. From the sound of her voice, she's eager to talk and to see you again."

"I always liked her."

"Apparently the feeling is mutual."

Susan picked up a biscuit and took a bite, and she had to admit, it did put her packaged-mix pancakes to shame. She finished it off and licked the crumbs from her fingers. Breakfast was the one meal she usually skipped, but this morning she was starving. The night's exercise had been good for her appetite as well as her heart.

"You better get moving," Jack warned. "We don't want to be late for the appointment, and we have a long drive back."

She swallowed the last of the coffee. "It will only take me a few minutes. I just need to grab a quick shower."

Susan adjusted the water, letting it run until it was comfortably hot. She stepped out of her robe and under the spray. Wet and warm, she ran her fingers down the flesh of her stomach and along her thighs.

Last night Jack had touched her like that, only his touch had left her burning with desire. Had he awakened this morning thinking about how it had felt to make love to her last night? Or had he only thought of calling the nurse and finding out everything he could about J. J. Darby?

It amazed her how he shifted from one part of his life

to another, setting each inside circles that never seemed to overlap. It was a skill she'd never learned, never needed until Rebecca and Timmy had come to live with her. Before that, her professional life had been the only one she had.

Soaping the cloth, she ran it over her body, coating her skin with a layer of frothy suds. Still, it would have been good for her ego to know that Jack hadn't been able to totally set aside his memories of last night. A word, a look, a touch. Anything more than the perfunctory kiss he'd given her would be nice.

She spun around as the shower curtain slid open and Jack stepped in behind her. Without a word, he pulled her to him, the water splashing over their heads and running in bubbling rivulets between their bodies.

"So you didn't forget me," she said, finding his lips.

He kissed her, warm and wet and wild, and the passion she'd thought well spent last night roared to life.

"No use to waste water," he said, his voice husky with desire. His mouth traced a path down her neck, and he cupped her breasts in his hands, pushing them up and tracing the nipples with his tongue.

"I'm all soapy," Susan said, her voice caught in the breath that held in her throat.

"You're right." He moved lower, down her stomach, his fingers and tongue like a torch against her skin. Moans of pleasure tore at her throat, and her insides quaked until she thought she might erupt with her need of him.

"Oh, Susan, Susan. What will I do about you? You make me forget the few rules I have." He straightened and pulled her to him. His hands were trembling as he guided himself inside her and claimed her once again.

But all Susan knew was that for the first time in her

life she had bonded intimately with another person, not just physically, but emotionally as well. And nothing had ever felt this good before.

NURSE BAILES'S house was set a good half acre from the road, nestled in a clump of pines a few yards from the lake where bream and catfish were said to be plentiful. Jack imagined they were, judging from the long dock that jutted into the gray water and the two fishing boats that looked ready to go at a moment's notice.

Before he stopped the car, the welcoming committee the nurse had warned him about showed up. Two Dobermans, the size of small horses, dared him to open the door.

"They look ferocious. Do you think they bite?" Susan asked.

"Either that or they're proud of their molars."

This time Jack followed instructions, tooting his horn and waiting until Mrs. Bailes came to the door and called the dogs. Even then he stepped out cautiously. The petite, middle-aged woman didn't seem too brave herself where the dogs were concerned.

She ushered Jack and Susan inside the house and thankfully shut the dogs outside. Her friendly drawl followed them down a narrow hall and into a spacious glass-enclosed room. The view was spectacular. Sunbeams danced in flickering formations of gold across the surface of the blue-green lake. But there were several downed limbs lying in her yard, the remnants of last night's ice storm.

"Your husband must be a fisherman," Jack said, admiring a huge bass mounted over the fireplace.

"We both are. The bass was my catch. I brought him in last year over at Toledo Bend."

"Nice catch." He read the inscription under the fish. "Beats my best by more than a pound."

The nurse walked to a table near the window and held up a carafe. "Would anyone like coffee?"

They both answered yes, and Jack waited until she'd poured three cups and set the tray of coffee, spoons, sugar and cream on the table in front of them. A cozy little party. It was time to liven it up.

"So, Mrs. Bailes, I'd like you to tell me about J. J. Darby. I understand he was sent to another facility when he tried to kill you."

"Call me Jessie," she said in the same friendly tone, but the smile vanished from her face. She stopped stirring her coffee and set the cup back on the table. "He's escaped, you know." Deep grooves settled around her eyes, as her expression grew grim. "I've lived in fear since the day I heard about it. That's why we bought the dogs."

"Has he tried to contact you?" Jack asked, his mind homing in on every nuance of her responses.

"Yes, he called here about a month ago. I was home alone."

"What did he say?"

"He said I had turned against him, and that he had to kill me."

"Did he say why?"

"Not this time. But when he attacked me in the Center, he claimed I was in league with Kelsey McKnight, and that we had conspired to keep him locked away when he'd never been found guilty."

"Tell us about his behavior patterns," Susan encouraged. "Anything you can remember."

The room was toasty warm, but Jessie shivered and wrapped her arms across her chest. She stared out the window a few seconds before she turned back to Susan. "J.J. was whatever he wanted to be. He could convince most people that he was as sane as they were until they got to know him. He'd go for weeks, laughing and joking with me, and then he'd change in an instant. He'd say something horribly vile in the same tone he'd used to joke with me. He could make my blood run cold, and he knew it."

"Was there any particular event or situation that would set him off?"

"Change. Any type of change in scheduling or sometimes in the weather. Most of the time it was Kelsey who bore the brunt of his obscene behaviors."

"Why didn't Dr. McKnight send him away earlier?" Jack asked.

"Kelsey thought Darby was making progress, that he was going longer and longer between his wild spells."

"My father thought he could cure even the most violent offenders," Susan said, turning to Jack.

"And he frequently did," Jessie said.

"What other characteristics did you notice about Darby?" Susan asked. "What did he like to do?"

Jessie sipped her coffee and stared into space. "Darby is a brilliant man. He was always cooking up elaborate schemes to lead the other inmates into trouble. He had a way of getting people to do whatever he wanted them to."

Jack scribbled furiously in his notebook and then turned back to Jessie. "How was he able to attack you? There must be precautions taken to prevent the inmates from attacking the staff."

"There are. Whenever the inmates are in the open areas, the guards are there. But J.J. got past the guard and hid outside the drug room. When I unlocked the door and went inside to prepare the evening medications, he followed me. He had a cord he'd found in the kitchen, the tie from a box of fruit that had been delivered that morning. One that should have been accounted for and destroyed.''

''So, he tried to strangle you.'' Susan said.

''Yes, and he would have succeeded if I hadn't been able to grab one of the needles from the tray I'd prepared. I plunged it into his arm. In the split second it took him to yank it out, I broke away from him and managed to escape.'' Jessie lowered her head and massaged both temples. ''I just want it to be over. I want him caught before he comes back to finish what he started with me. And before he hurts someone else.''

''If I have anything to say about it, he will be,'' Jack promised. ''Can you give me a description of him?''

''I can do better than that. I have a snapshot that was taken at Guest and Visitor Day just before the attack. I had it duplicated so that I could give copies to the local lawmen. I can give you a copy if you like.''

''That would be a great help.''

She left the room for only a few seconds. When she returned, she carried the picture between two fingers, as if she could barely stand to touch it. She handed it to Jack.

He studied the details. The man's head was shaved and his face was half hidden under a scraggy beard. He looked to be about forty-five, medium build, no signs of scars or tattoos.

''How tall was he?''

''Five feet ten and a half inches, and he weighed a hundred and eighty-five pounds. I know exactly. I took his height and weight the week before he tried to kill me. I remember the day well. He'd been laughing and teasing me about how I got to check out all the men. The next minute he was describing how he'd like to wrap his hands around my neck and kill me."

"A real Jekyll and Hyde," Jack commented.

"Exactly. He's the type of a man who can appear normal one minute and turn deadly in the blink of an eye."

"If I recall correctly, that was pretty much what I told the judge years ago," Susan said. "I never had a minute's doubt I'd made the right recommendation about J.J. He was never mentally fit to stand trial."

"Or to walk free," Jack added, tapping his pencil on his notebook. "But he is."

The questioning continued for another hour, but little new information was revealed. It was difficult for Jack to buy that this man could possibly be tied in with Gabriel, but stranger things had happened. Two facts Jack had learned in his years with the NOPD. Never turn your back on danger, and never close your mind to any possibility.

He wasn't taking any chances. No matter what the Chief said, this case would not be closed nor Susan and the children's protection ended until he was sure the right man was in jail. Not even if he had to twist a few arms and call in some favors to make sure they were never left unguarded.

Jack broke into the conversation, thanking Jessie again for her help. She walked them to the car, while the dogs sat under a tree watching them.

Nice guard dogs, but Jack wouldn't give two cents for the protection they'd offer against a man like J.J.

Jessie shook his hand and hugged Susan. "Oh," she said, breaking away from the hug. "I almost forgot to tell you. When I was cleaning out your father's old office closet the other day, I found a box of notes and letters you'd sent him. Would you like to have them?''

"You mean he kept them?"

"Hundreds of them. Some of the cards were ones you'd made him in grade school. I can have them shipped to you if you'd like."

"Thanks, Jessie. I think I would like to have them." Susan brushed a hand across her eyes, and Jack saw the moisture gathering in their depths. Yet another side of Susan McKnight.

He squeezed her hand and then rounded the car, got in behind the wheel and, putting the key in the ignition, brought the car to life. Six hours and no mishaps and they'd be home.

And with any luck, by that time someone would have located J. J. Darby. Every police department in the state had already been put on the alert. In a few hours, they'd also have a picture.

But physical appearances could change rapidly, and usually did when a man was on the run. Clean-shaven, with a full head of hair, Darby would look like a different man.

Jack picked up the cellular phone and punched in Casanova's number. The detective answered immediately, but he had nothing of interest to share. This time no news was not good news. In spite of the all-points-bulletin that had gone out yesterday, there was no record of anyone having seen Darby since he'd ridden a laundry truck out of the hospital.

*7:00 p.m.*

JACK SAT AT HIS DESK with a cup of tepid coffee and a cold oyster po'boy at his elbow.

"I thought I might catch you here," Casanova said, stepping in the door and tossing a stack of papers on Jack's desk. "I got a very interesting phone call concerning Bobby Chambers while you toured the great white north with the dragon lady."

"And?"

"The caller was none other than Mr. Gregory Taylor." Casanova pulled out his pocket notebook and read. "In light of recent news developments, he felt it necessary to inform us that Dr. McKnight's secretary, Mr. Bobby Chambers, called him three weeks ago offering to provide him with information about his wife's indiscretions in exchange for cash."

"You don't say. Put out a little cheese and all the rats come out."

"I don't know how this fits in with Hornsby's killing two women, but it makes interesting material for the case file."

"I'd say it does." Jack grabbed his coat. "Come on, Casanova, let's go calling."

"I guess that rules out the dinner I was about to go eat."

"Unless Bobby Chambers invites us to dine with him."

*7:10 p.m.*

BOBBY CHAMBERS LOCKED the office door and looked around to see if anyone was watching him leave. Satisfied that the streets were clear, he ran to his car.

Everything had happened so fast. He hadn't even had a chance to cash the check in his pocket. He didn't dare do it now.

Sweat popped out on Bobby's forehead in spite of the

temperature. He slid behind the wheel of his car and started the engine. He had some business that had to be taken care of tonight. The first stop would be at the home of his boss.

# Chapter Twelve

"Auntie Mom, what time do we need to leave if we have to be at City Park by eight?"

The bowl of leftovers Susan was sliding into the refrigerator wobbled in her hands. She'd completely forgotten Rebecca's class was singing carols tonight at Celebration in the Oaks.

She and Jack hadn't made it back from North Louisiana until four, which meant she'd had to cancel an entire day's appointments. And the natives were restless. She'd returned phone calls and agreed to see the two patients tonight who'd put up the biggest fuss. Now it was either disappoint Rebecca or call and cancel them again.

"We'd have to leave in about fifteen minutes, and it's very cold outside. Would you rather stay here and watch your new Christmas movie?"

"I don't mind the cold. I can wear my hat and gloves and everything. Anyway, they need me to sing. My teacher says I have strong vocal cords."

"Your teacher is right."

The eager look on Rebecca's face made saying no to her very difficult. But work couldn't be put off. Maybe Lucy and the guard-dog cop could take them.

"Missy Sippen's whole family's going to come and hear her sing, aunts and uncles and everybody," Rebecca said, pushing wayward bangs out of her face. "But I told her I only need you, Auntie Mom."

Okay, that settled it. If her two demanding patients had a true emergency, she'd see them later, midnight if she had to, but she was not going to let Rebecca down this time. After all, it was Christmas.

Good grief. Now she was starting to sound like Jack.

Susan left the dirty dishes stacked in the sink and hurriedly called her two determined patients, offering to meet them for late-night appointments. They both turned her down. New Orleans was a city where celebrating started late in the evening, and both of them had other plans they didn't want to change.

Susan's guilt diminished greatly. If their problems weren't significant enough for them to miss a holiday party, then they certainly weren't significant enough for Susan to miss Rebecca's concert. She stopped at the mirror and smoothed on some lipstick and a touch of blush, taking an extra few seconds to tuck escaping hairs back under the control of her pearl barrette.

"You'll do," she said to the reflection in the mirror, and "do" was good enough. Rebecca was the prima donna tonight. Grabbing a tissue to blot her lips, she ran to help Rebecca dress in her white cotton blouse with the Peter Pan collar and her red velvet skirt, the one they had bought on their last shopping adventure.

A few minutes of pushing, pulling and tucking and Rebecca twirled to watch her full skirt bell out around her short legs. She did look like a holiday doll, Susan decided. She hugged her, and Rebecca hugged back.

Tonight should be special. A treat for all of them after the horrors of the last few days. Not that Rebecca and Timmy knew about the murders or even the notes, but they knew she'd been upset. And they were well aware that there was always at least one stranger in the house.

Both Rebecca and Timmy had questioned her about the visitors. Susan had explained the police officers away as some friends of her father who needed a place to stay for a few days. At three, Timmy took her at her word, but Rebecca clearly had her doubts.

"Up on the housetop…"

Susan left the room as Rebecca put her strong vocal cords to work. "It's your turn, Timmy," she said, stopping to turn off the television set. "Let's get ready to go."

"No, I don't wanna hear Rebecca sing."

"Sure you do. Your sister's a very good singer and has strong vocal cords." Susan took his chubby hand and led him to the bathroom. "I'll bet Missy Sippen's brother will be there. And after Rebecca sings, you can ride the carousel."

His eyes lit up. "Can I ride a big horse?"

"The biggest one they have. And then we can ride a train through trees decorated with millions of Christmas lights."

"A real train with a whistle?" He demonstrated the shrill whistling to be sure Susan understood.

"Yes, a real train with a whistle, but it's a miniature."

"What's that?"

"It means it's smaller than regular trains. This one runs through the park and it was made especially for children."

"And big boys?"

"And big boys like you. Even adults can ride, so I can sit next to you."

"What about Santa?"

"I imagine he'll be at the North Pole making toys. It's only three days until Christmas, you know."

"Not *that* Santa. *Our* Santa."

"Oh, Jack. No, I don't think he'll be there tonight. He has work to do." She combed Timmy's hair and straightened his shirt. "You look mighty handsome," she said, kissing his cheek.

"As handsome as Detective Santa?"

"You really like him, don't you, Timmy?"

"Yes. Don't you?"

"Yes, Timmy. I like him. I like him a whole lot."

Susan went to get the children's coats and hats from the closet, but the last part of her talk with Timmy replayed in her mind. She more than liked Jack. She was in love with him.

But when this was over, where would she be? Alone, reliving the passion he'd awakened? Missing him? Climbing back into her protective shell, more afraid than ever of involvement and intimacy. She'd made her choice, and if it came to that, she'd handle it.

But what about the kids? They'd already lost so much. Was it fair to bring him into their lives the way she had the last few days? Decorating the Christmas tree, taking them for a ride in the carriage, even reading them stories and tucking them into bed. They had already lost the two most important people in their lives.

Rebecca skipped into the room singing the chorus to "Jingle Bells," and Susan forced a smile to her lips. "I think it's time for us to get you and your strong vocal cords to the park."

"Yes, ma'am." Rebecca twirled one last time before settling down long enough to don her coat and hat.

Susan let Officer Hammonds know it was time to leave and then helped Rebecca and Timmy get their coats buttoned straight and their hats tied tight. It was only a short walk to the covered parking space behind the courtyard where she kept the car, but they would need their coats to stay warm at the outdoor concert.

Tonight should be a special night, Susan reminded herself, as they marched out the back door, accompanied by Betty Hammonds. That meant she had to keep unpleasant thoughts at bay for a couple of hours. No trying to second-guess Jack's intentions, and no thinking about killers.

Of course, that would be a little hard to do with a bodyguard at her side.

"Dr. McKnight, wait!"

She turned as Bobby Chambers chased her across the back courtyard. "What are you doing back here?"

"I came this way so I could see if your car was here," he explained. "It was, and the gate wasn't locked, so I cut through the back way." He nodded toward the narrow passage between two apartments that connected the courtyard to the side street.

"Is something wrong?" She tried to lower her voice and disguise the panic. She did a poor job. Hammonds moved in closer, and Bobby glared at her suspiciously. Susan had no choice but to offer introductions.

"This is Betty Hammonds, a friend of my late father's. She's staying with me for a few days."

They exchanged handshakes, and Bobby turned back to Susan. "Nothing's happened, at least nothing that has to do with business, but I need to talk to you. It's important."

"Unless we can have this talk in sixty seconds, Bobby, we'll have to make it later. Rebecca's class is singing at Celebration in the Oaks tonight, and I'm afraid traffic will be backed up getting into City Park."

"My class sings at 8:30, but we have to be there at 8:00. You can come and hear me, if you want to."

"Not tonight, Rebecca. Tonight I have to talk to your mother."

Susan detected an urgency in Bobby's voice that set her nerves on edge. "I wish I could stay and talk now, Bobby, but I can't."

He stepped closer. "Why don't you let me drive you to the park? Mrs. Hammonds can take the children in your car and you can meet them there."

Susan was on the verge of agreeing when she looked up and met Betty Hammonds' warning stare. "I can't, Bobby. Not tonight." His face fell, and she put a hand on his arm. "I'm truly sorry. Can we talk later?"

"I guess I have no choice."

Shoulders slumped, he walked back the way he'd come. A couple of lead weights settled on Susan's shoulders. Complications, demands, desires, and danger were ganging up against her. Something would have to give soon.

She climbed into the car and waited until everyone had buckled up before backing onto the street and into the line of early-evening traffic.

Maybe a night of carols and the glow of a million lights shining from the tops of century-old oak trees would be just what she needed. That and a night without any notes from party crashers.

A sigh escaped her lips. It was almost too much to hope for.

SUSAN SAT IN THE second row, surrounded by parents and grandparents, all listening to the off-key performance by the first graders.

Timmy slid from his folding chair to the cold ground, pretending that he'd fallen. He'd been as good as gold for the first twenty minutes of the concert, but his ability to sit still had run its course. She nodded to Officer Hammonds and took Timmy's hand, leading him to the area behind the folding chairs. Hammonds followed.

"This is some display," Hammonds commented. "I've never been out here during the Christmas season before. I'd heard about Celebration in the Oaks, but I had no idea it was so impressive."

"And this is just a small part of it," Susan said, as Timmy pulled her within touching distance of a spruce tree that had been decorated by one of the local schools. "There's a driving tour that winds for miles beneath an oak archway of lighted stars, angels, candles and other Christmas symbols. And then there's the walking tour. A virtual fairyland."

"I'll have to get back out here before the season's over."

"It's practically bright as day out here with all the lights, and there are people everywhere. If you like you could take the walking tour while we stand in line to ride the carousel and miniature train."

Hammonds shook her head, her frustration obvious. "Don't even think about it, Susan. It may be light where we're standing right now, but there are pockets of darkness all over this park. There's no way of knowing who's watching from around any corner."

Susan pulled her jacket around her, suddenly cold and wary. Perhaps it was just the power of suggestion, but it was as if she could feel someone watching her, feel the presence of an evil that shouldn't be here in this place of beauty and peace.

She reached down and picked up Timmy and carried him closer so that she could hear the last few songs of the concert. She needed the message of the carols to ease the anxiety that gripped her heart. Gabriel was in jail. The nightmare was supposed to be over, but the presence of Hammonds at her side told her Jack was not convinced that it was.

Gabriel and Darby. The psychopath and the surgeon. The man who'd killed his parents, and the man whose life had been shaped by his mother's infidelities.

It might be possible they had joined in some bizarre murderous scheme, but it was easier to believe that Santa Claus was real and that his reindeer really did poop on roofs. Still, something was wrong. Or at least, Jack thought so. The presence of Hammonds was proof of that.

THE LINE FOR THE TRAIN ride stretched around the roped-off loop twice and out to the back gate by the time Susan, the children and Officer Hammonds took their places at the end.

"Why don't I step to the stand over there and get hot chocolate for all of us while you and the kids hold our place in line," Susan said, sure her offer would be rejected.

Hammonds stared at the stand for a minute and then scanned the area behind them. "You stay here," she said. "I'll get the chocolate and be right back."

Uneasiness twitched in Susan's stomach as Hammonds set off in the opposite direction. It eased quickly. Hammonds made a stop to chat with the uniformed policeman standing between them and the gate. He nodded and smiled in Susan's direction.

Double coverage. She and the children couldn't be safer, but the conversation with Jessie still haunted her mind. John Jasper Darby, a man on the loose who oscillated between charming gentleman and ruthless killer.

She remembered the original trial and the evaluation the judge had requested. She had assisted her father, but he'd pretty much left that one to her. One of the few times she'd felt he trusted her judgment. Later, she'd learned he had no choice but to depend on her. He'd been ill that week, suffering from a heart condition he'd never told her about. The one that eventually took his life.

"The line's moving. We might get on this time," Rebecca chirped.

"I don't think so, sweetie. There's a lot of people in front of us."

"We can't leave Mrs. Hammonds," Timmy protested. "She has the chocolate."

"Ho, ho, ho. Merry Christmas!"

"It's Santa," Timmy squealed, running toward the red-suited man approaching them.

Susan smiled. She recognized the "ho." In seconds, the fat man was surrounded by not only Rebecca and Timmy but dozens of children, tugging on his suit and telling him what they wanted for Christmas. He passed out candy canes to all of them and gave high fives and a couple of kisses to pink-cheeked babies.

Hammonds returned with the chocolate just as the line started moving again. Rebecca and Timmy came tearing back, not willing to lose their place in line even for Santa.

Jack followed them. He kissed Susan on the cheek,

and the children who were watching his every move burst into giggles.

"And what do you want, little girl?"

"A sane man."

"You wouldn't like him," he whispered in her ear. "Sane men never take rides on roller coasters."

"You really do work at the mall when you're off duty, don't you? They probably don't even have to pay you."

"Pay? You mean people get money for this?"

She shook her head in hopelessness and sipped her chocolate. Last night she'd been naked in bed with this man. Love definitely addled the brain.

Rebecca reached up and took Jack's hand. "Will you ride the train with us, Santa?"

"I don't have a ticket."

Hammonds poked hers at him. "You take mine, and I'll go take the walking tour. I'm sure I'm not needed around here anymore."

"As a matter of fact," Jack said, "you can have the rest of the night off. I'll stay on duty until your replacement arrives. But stay where I can get you if something comes up and I have to run."

Run, as in to the scene of another murder. Susan didn't miss his meaning. The lines dividing Jack's two worlds were becoming blurred. Only they'd never been separate, except in Susan's mind. She understood that now.

Santa suits and murders, kisses and clues, making love and interrogating. All part of the complex human being who was Jack Carter. So where did a quiet, predictable psychologist fit into his world? Part of the excitement, or merely a means to solve the top-priority case? Or was it all one and the same to him?

The line moved again, and they were herded through

the turnstile. Rebecca and Timmy jumped aboard and ran to the first available seat. Jack and Susan squeezed in beside them. Seconds later the whistle blew, the train moved out of the station, and everybody's eyes grew wide in wonder.

The rickety wooden train itself was a sight to behold. Each open car was outlined in garlands of sparkling lights. They rode the rough railroad ties past the antique carousel and through a joyful scene of other turning, twisting carnival rides. Children and grown-ups alike waved to them as they chugged by, and Santa, Timmy and Rebecca waved back to everyone.

The train blew its whistle loudly as it crossed a park road. They moved beyond the crowds of people and into a Christmas wonderland accompanied by a constant chorus of oohs and ahs.

"Look, there's reindeer," Timmy said, pointing to a a spot under the trees where several lighted specimens stood beside a toy-filled sleigh.

"And look at that tree," Rebecca chanted. "It's taller than our house." It was, covered in twinkling splendor and topped with a silver star.

They crossed a pond where lighted frogs jumped on cue and a bright green alligator moved across the waters, all fake and harmless and shimmering in the moonlight like diamonds.

"Look over there, Auntie Mom, there's baby Jesus," Timmy crooned, pointing to a life-sized nativity up ahead, complete with painted wooden camels and wise men bearing gifts. The train slowed for everyone to admire the works of art and then disappeared under a shower of millions of twinkling lights as they rode under the famed archway.

"I'm glad I caught up with you in time for this," Jack

said nestling her under his arm and against his fur-trimmed chest.

"How did you find us?" she asked.

"You can never run from the long arms of the law."

"Hammonds called you, didn't she, and told you where we would be."

"You don't let a man have any secrets, do you?"

It wasn't true. She was certain Jack had many secrets, that he told her only what he thought she had to know.

She looked up as the man-made lights above them disappeared, letting the real stars and a full moon shine through the bare branches of the magnificent trees. Celebration in the Oaks, a perfect name for the wonders all around them.

But even splendor such as that couldn't fully override the thoughts that had wormed their way back into her mind. "Did you find out anything more about Darby this afternoon?" she asked, as the train neared the station.

"Not yet," he whispered, "all I want to think about now is you." He tucked a thumb under her chin and tilted her face upward.

She stared into his eyes. They gleamed from the reflection of bright, twinkling lights, but were still shaded with desire.

"Merry Christmas, Susan." He touched his lips to hers and she melted in his arms, unaware that the train had stopped until the passengers around her erupted in cheers.

She jerked away from him, her face on fire from the mother of all blushes.

"Auntie Mom, you kissed Santa Claus," Timmy exclaimed.

"Santa knows a good thing when he sees it, Timmy," Jack answered.

"Can we ride one more time?" Rebecca begged. "There's no school tomorrow."

Timmy joined in the chorus. "Yes, can we please, just one more time?"

"The line is too long," Susan explained. "Besides, once is enough."

Rebecca's bottom lip jutted out and she gave Susan her most pitiful, imploring gaze. Timmy just looked longingly at the train that was already loading with the next round of excited passengers.

Jack leaned over and whispered in her ear. "You didn't think once was enough last night."

"Oh, good grief. I give up." She turned her back on all of them and marched to the back of the line, but she was no longer cold. Just the mention of last night had warmed her considerably.

SUSAN HELPED TIMMY with his seat belt while Jack and Rebecca climbed out of the car. Both Timmy and Rebecca were well aware by now that the Santa in their car was Jack, but it hadn't dimmed the magic for either of them. The logic of believing in Santa, even when you knew who the man in the red suit really was, escaped Susan, but apparently neither Rebecca nor Timmy had a problem with it.

"I hope you have a change of clothes," she said, as she locked the car.

"Sure. Santas and Boy Scouts always come prepared. You should know that. I have a well stocked duffel in my car."

"And where would that be, at City Park?"

"Parked in the tow-away zone in front of your house."

"How do you get away with that? If I park there for five minutes, I get a ticket."

"It's all in knowing the right people."

"I think I should call Bobby Chambers," she said, as they walked across the courtyard to her back door.

Jack took her elbow. "Business at this time of night?"

"I'm not sure. He came by the house just as we were leaving tonight. He said he had something important to talk to me about. When I couldn't stay, he looked upset."

Jack nodded his head, his mind chasing through a pack of new possibilities. That's why he and Casanova hadn't found Bobby at the office, at home, or at his favorite table at the casino.

Jack tugged Susan to a stop while the kids ran on ahead. "Invite him over, but before he gets here, I need to fill you in on a few new details about him."

"Look, Auntie Mom. Someone brought us flowers." Rebecca stopped in front of a large pot of poinsettias that hadn't been at their back door when they'd left.

"Don't touch it," Jack ordered.

"Why?" Rebecca looked at him quizzically. "It's just flowers. They can't hurt you."

Susan moved between Rebecca and the plant. "They might not be ours. We have to see if there's a card."

Jack knew Susan suspected the same thing he did. He stooped, parting the blossoms and searching between the stems and leaves for a note. Nothing. He lifted the plant and walked his fingers across the bottom of the clay pot. Perfectly clean.

"Looks like a gift from a neighbor," he said.

Susan's sigh of relief was audible. "It's probably from Lucy. She's so thoughtful. Now let's get inside. I know two children who are up way past their bedtimes."

Susan unlocked the door and the four of them tramped in. Poinsettias in the courtyard, a decorated tree in the apartment, and laughter in the air. It must be Christmas, but it was like no Christmas she'd ever known.

Even with all she'd been through the last few days, happiness warmed her insides like a cozy fire. Surely, Jack had been right. Gabriel had been behind the notes and the murders. He was a sick man, but he was getting help. And her party crasher had obviously gone on to other parties.

And as for J. J. Darby, he didn't stand a chance. Detective Jack Carter was on his trail, and he always got his man. And, this time, if he wanted her, he'd also gotten a woman.

"I'll put the kids to bed and then you can tell me the latest about Bobby," Susan said, shrugging out of her coat.

"Auntie Mom, look, someone left me a present." Rebecca ran into the kitchen, a small square package in her hand. The wrapping paper was identical to the paper used on the gift that had been left on her porch two nights ago.

"Where did you get that?"

"It was on my bed."

Terror rose inside Susan, mingling with a deeper anger than she'd ever known. Some rotten coward had broken into her home while she was gone, walked into Rebecca's room and left his disgusting handiwork. No doubt another note.

"If this is the party crasher, Jack, I want you to catch him and let *me* crash *him* with my bare hands." The words were low, spoken threw clenched teeth.

"What party?"

"No party, Rebecca. It's time for bed."

"But I want to open my present."

"It's not a present, sweetie. It's a joke. A very bad joke."

Susan threw the package at Jack and went to help Timmy get into his pajamas. The note could wait until she'd read bedtime stories and gotten her hugs. Then maybe she'd be calm enough to face it without screaming.

## Chapter Thirteen

Once the children were in bed, Susan had no more excuses for avoiding the dreadful note. She walked into the kitchen. Jack was already on the phone, barking orders, the unwrapped package gripped tightly in his hand. She put out her hand for it, but he waved her away.

She dropped to a kitchen chair and waited. "So what does this note say?" she asked, when he hung up the phone.

"It was more than a note. This time a gift was included."

The tone of Jack's voice and the strained lines in his face told her the stakes had just changed.

"What kind of gift?"

Jack took the lid off the box and pulled out a bright yellow scarf. The silk fabric waved in the air, exuding the familiar, nauseating scent, and every muscle in Susan's body tightened.

"Why would someone do this?"

"I'm not sure what's going on here, Susan, but we have to tighten security again."

"I already have a guard inside my home and one at the office. I don't know how much tighter we can get unless I sleep with one."

"We're going to reinstate a stakeout team to watch your apartment at all times. I want to know everyone who comes near here. The person who delivered this package tonight likely has a key. I've already checked the windows and doors for break-in. There isn't a sign."

Fingers of fear clutched at her lungs. "You don't think this is a hoax anymore, do you, Jack?"

"Read the note, Susan. Then we'll talk."

Hesitantly, she picked up the sheet of paper.

Dr. McKnight,
The game is nearly over. I promised you that before Christmas you would be begging me for mercy. You must realize by now that I plan to keep my word. Before that time, you may want to thank your friends. They have all been extremely helpful to me. I hope you made peace with your father, Susan. You'll see him soon.
J. J. Darby

"Darby." Dread settled like lead in her stomach.

"It looks that way. I don't take anything for granted in this case. Someone who knows we went to the Center to check out Darby could have typed his name to throw us off base."

"You don't believe that. I can see it in your eyes." She dropped the note to the table. "At least you don't have to look for him anymore, Jack. Just wait here. He'll come to me. Before Christmas."

"Not a chance." He pulled her to her feet and wrapped his arms about her. "We'll assign every available officer to comb the French Quarter night and day. If Darby is behind this, he has to be somewhere in this area."

"You could look for months and not find him. We have three days at the most."

"That's why we're covering all the bases. This afternoon, I questioned Maggie Henderson's best friend and also one of the women she was close to at work."

"What did you expect to get from them?"

"To see if they've ever seen her with a man who resembles Darby."

"Had they?"

"They gave me a couple of long shots. Thorough background checks are being run on both of them as we speak. Someone else questioned Gabriel, but he's either not talking or is still too out of it to know anything. Believe me, Susan, we aren't a bunch of impotent puppets, waiting for this lunatic to pull our strings."

Susan pulled away from Jack. "Top priority, all the resources of the NOPD at work, and one unstable man is still winning."

"He may be ahead. He's not winning."

Susan walked to the sink and started loading the dinner dishes into the dishwasher. She had to do something with her hands to keep from pounding them into the wall. "Why, me, Jack? After seven years, why me?"

"Who knows what's festered in a mind like that. And it doesn't really matter now. What matters is that we find him. And we will." He started to pace. "There's one other thing I need to tell you, Susan."

"More good news?"

"You may not think so. I have a man staked out near Bobby Chambers' apartment. I want him picked up for questioning the second he shows up."

"What could Bobby possibly have to do with Darby?"

"We said the same thing about Gabriel, but it looks

like we were wrong. Besides, the note says to thank your friends for helping him. My guess is Darby's gotten to somebody besides Gabriel. It could well be Chambers.''

''I still don't see how Bobby fits into this. I hired him through a reputable agency. He didn't come to me. I went looking for him.''

''Does he have a key to your apartment?''

''No.''

''Not that you know of. But how difficult would it have been for him to slip your keys from your pocket or handbag and have one made? He could have had the original back in place before you missed it.''

Susan raked her hair back with shaky fingers. ''I just don't get it, Jack. This doesn't compute.''

''I'm examining all possibilities. You told me a few nights ago that you thought someone had been in your apartment one day while you were out. You had noticed that sweet smelling aftershave that nauseates you.''

''Yes, but not just a whiff or a faint scent like the one left on the notes and on the scarves. The apartment reeked of it. Even Rebecca and Timmy noticed it. We decided one of the neighbors was cooking something really foul for dinner.''

''But you've never noticed the smell on Chambers?''

''No, not once. I don't believe Bobby's involved in this.''

''Don't count him out. There's more.''

''Why am I not surprised?''

She listened as Jack told her about the phone call from Gregory Taylor saying Bobby had offered to sell him information about his wife's infidelities. The news hurt deep inside. She'd trusted Bobby, almost as much as she trusted Lucy.

Jack walked over and stood behind her. He wrapped

his hands around her waist and rocked her against him. He hated to leave her tonight, but he had no choice. He had to be out working on the case or go crazy himself. Somewhere in the city of New Orleans, there had to be answers.

He buried his face in Susan's silky hair and then moved his lips to her ear. "The first night I met you, I called you the dragon lady," he whispered.

"You called me what?"

"The dragon lady. You know, armor-plated, breathing fire."

She twisted in his arms so that she could look into his eyes. "And now you've changed your mind about me?"

"No way." He kissed the end of her nose. "Now I know you're a dragon lady."

"The night we met." Susan held tightly to Jack. "It seems like a lifetime ago."

"No, we still have lots of living to do. I'm not nearly ready to climb off the roller coaster, not after last night. But it's late. Why don't you get ready for bed? I'll call Hammonds back in to take over for me."

She pulled away from him. "You can't go back to work tonight, Jack. You had so little sleep last night."

"You did keep me busy." He smiled and kissed her again, this time on the mouth. He pulled away reluctantly. "But I have a few things I want to check on. You go ahead and get some rest. I'll be here until Hammonds comes."

"No, while we're waiting, we should be working together on this. I hold to my original idea. Why look for Darby? He wants me. He'll come after me, so we set a trap."

"He's too unpredictable. *Traps* are too unpredictable. The best bet is always to catch the bad guys off guard and make an arrest. Not that I don't intend to have you protected every second. I do.''

''Then let's get back to the friends concept.''

Jack stared at her in amazement. In the last few minutes she'd received a note saying she'd be killed in the next three days, signed by a man she knew was capable of cold-blooded murder. Now she was standing here planning out strategies as if she'd been given a puzzle to solve.

A dragon lady. No doubt about it.

They worked until Hammonds arrived. While Susan got ready for bed, Jack went over the newest note with his fellow officer. He discussed in detail the special procedures he wanted her to follow. No one except Lucy Carmichael was to enter the house without his approval. If anything unusual occurred, or if Bobby Chambers showed up, he was to be notified at once.

Hammonds assured him everything was under control. She'd already been in contact with the police unit assigned to that area. They would respond to a call from her immediately. And the stakeout team Jack had requested for the outside of the house would be in place by midnight. If Darby, or anyone else up to no good, showed his face, he was as good as caught.

Jack went to the bedroom to tell Susan good-night. She had changed into a silky pink nightshirt and let down her hair. She patted the spot next to where she was propped against a bank of pillows. He took the seat, knowing he shouldn't. It would make it that much harder to leave.

She ran a finger down his arm. ''Call me if anything changes.''

''I'll keep you posted. And don't worry. Everything's under control. Detective Santa's in charge.'' He leaned over and kissed her, stopping only because he had to. "I have to get out of here while I still can."

She gave him a playful shove. He started out, but her voice stopped him before he reached the door.

"Jack."

He looked back. "Yeah?"

She shook her head as if she'd changed her mind about what she wanted to say. "Just be careful," she whispered. "I want you back."

*Thursday, December 23*
*4:00 a.m.*

BOBBY CHAMBERS SAT in the bar in the heart of the Irish Channel. He was drunk, and he was in big trouble. "One more beer," he said, when the bartender came by.

"You've had enough, buddy. Let me call you a cab."

"No, I got nowhere to go. My girlfriend dumped me, and my buddy got me in trouble so deep, I'd have to have a ladder to see daylight."

"A sad story. All the same, it's 4:00 a.m., closing time, and you're in no shape to drive home."

"Even my boss threw me out. I tried to talk to her, but she didn't have time to listen. She should have. Dr. Susan. Have you ever heard of her?"

"Can't say that I have. I stay away from doctors."

"I should have, too. At least I should have stayed away from her records. Now I know everything about everybody. Do you want to know who Gregory Taylor's wife sleeps with?"

"Well, I bet it's not you. You don't know Gregory Taylor or his wife. Now go home and sleep it off."

"I do so know him."

"Yeah, and I'm best friends with the mayor. He

comes over to my house in the Channel every night and we shoot the breeze about the city's problems."

"I know Gabriel Hornsby, too."

"The crazy doctor who strangled his wife? I guess you were his accomplice." The bartender broke into laughter and gave his bar one last swipe with the wet cloth.

"You don't think I know Gabriel Hornsby? I'll prove it to you." Bobby dug into his pocket and pulled out his billfold. He took the five-thousand-dollar check Gabriel had given him and spread it out on the bar, rubbing it with his fingers to remove the creases. His fingers kept sliding off the check. The paper was as slick as his barstool.

"Pick up your check, fellow. You already paid me, and you've had your last drink for tonight. Besides, I don't take anything but cash and plastic."

"Just come look at this check. It'll prove I know Gabriel Hornsby."

"Yeah, right. I called you a cab, and it'll be here any minute. Go on outside and wait on it. I'm locking up."

Bobby was leaving, but not in the cab. He still had one last piece of business to take care of.

He picked up his check and tried to put it back in his pocket. He missed, and the check drifted to the floor.

The bartender leaned over and picked it up for him. "Where'd you get this?"

"From the man you claim I don't know. He's my business partner, at least he was. Our deal is concluded."

"Yeah, well, let me hold it for you while you wait for the cab."

"I don't need a cab." Bobby tried to say more, but his mouth felt like a wad of cotton was stuck under his tongue, and he was getting very sleepy. He looked up to see the bartender walking away with his check.

"Hey, come back here with that. I earned every penny of it." The bartender paid him no mind. He was on the phone. Bobby put his head down on the bar. He didn't need a cab. He had to go see Dr. McKnight.

He closed his eyes. He needed to clear his head. But there was so much noise, blaring sirens loud enough to blow your head off. He raised his head to see two policemen barreling through the door and heading straight for him.

*8:00 a.m.*

JACK TOOK THE LAST bite of the greasy sausage biscuit he'd picked up on the way to the station. He'd only gotten a few hours' sleep last night, but he wasn't tired. He never was when a case was hot, and this one was scorching.

Bobby Chambers was in custody. Passed out from a late night of drinking, but he was there all the same. As soon as he became lucid, he had a lot of talking to do.

Casanova rushed into the room and dropped a new stack of computer printouts on top of Jack's other clutter. "You are going to love this."

"You found Darby?"

"It's not quite that good. Take a look at it." He leaned over and touched his finger to an item that had been circled in red. "Hornsby wrote not one but three checks to Bobby Chambers in the last four weeks. The first two were for a grand each. The third one, the one we have, was written two days before he killed his wife."

Casanova dropped to the chair on the other side of

Jack's desk and cocked it back, propping his feet on top of the Chief's latest memo. "Looks like you'll be busy today."

"Yeah, and I think I'll start with Bobby Chambers. He owes me lots of explanations."

"Do you need some help? We can do the good cop, bad cop routine. I'll be the bad guy."

"Of course. Me, I'm just the jovial Santa type."

"The plot definitely thickens," Casanova said. "I don't get it, though." He dropped his feet back to the floor. "If Gabriel was paying Chambers for information about Sherry, what's the deal with the notes? And who killed Maggie Henderson? And how in the devil would Darby fit into all of this?"

"I don't know, but I sure as hell plan to find out." Jack stood and shuffled papers around until he found his jacket under one of the piles. "Right now I'm paying a visit to central lockup."

"I guess that means you're not eating that biscuit."

Jack grabbed his breakfast just before Casanova swept down on it like the vulture he was. "I know it's hard for you to believe, buddy, limited as you are, but I can do two things at once. Like eat and drive."

"Limited? Is that any way to talk to a man who did the busywork all week while you kept company with the gorgeous dragon lady?"

"You're right. I owe you one, but not my breakfast." Jack headed out. "Are you coming or not, bad cop?"

*2:55 p.m.*

SUSAN'S MORNING had passed uneventfully. She'd come to her office as always, even though a madman had vowed to kill her. Sitting idle would have made her even more irritable and restless than she was already.

Going about her usual routine helped, but it didn't make her forget that Darby was probably lurking somewhere nearby, waiting for the opportunity to finish what he'd started. Especially when Simpson, a plainclothes officer with a loaded gun hidden beneath his stylish sports coat, sat in her reception area, scrutinizing every patient who walked through her door.

She'd called home after each session to make sure there had been no more notes and that everything was fine. It always was. This afternoon Lucy and the children were baking Christmas cookies. Before lunch, Lucy and the hopefully unobtrusive guard had taken them into the courtyard to play hopscotch and bounce balls.

Thanks to Lucy, the children's lives were *almost* normal. Thanks to Jack and the NOPD, Susan knew they were protected every second. Hammonds would be back on duty at three, only a few minutes away, and Lucy was looking forward to having the friendly female return.

The male cop working the day shift was much too stern and silent for Lucy's taste. Not only that, but he'd eaten half their cookies, and Lucy detested gluttons.

Wonderful Lucy. She was not only a caretaker for the children, but a special friend. She would have to think of something really nice to do for her when this nightmare was finally over.

*When? If?*

Two days until Christmas, but Susan was determined to keep planning as if the day might actually come and go without the promised catastrophe. This morning she'd ordered the beautiful, freckled doll from the store on Royal Street and had it delivered to her office. She hoped

Rebecca wouldn't be disappointed when what she really wanted didn't show up under the tree. Whatever that might be.

The only problem had been in the puppy department. She'd let her fingers walk the yellow pages, but the pet stores were sold out of small, friendly puppies suitable for a three-year-old who lived in a city apartment. The rest of her shopping had been completed long before her life had dissolved into a mass of fear and chaos.

*Before Christmas, you'll be begging me for mercy.*

Susan shivered as the words of the killer's note haunted her mind. John Jasper Darby planned to kill her. Jack planned to make sure he didn't. She'd put her money on Jack. Everything he'd promised, he'd delivered right on time.

The phone rang, and Susan picked up the receiver. "Hello."

"Susan, this is Lucy. We have a little emergency."

Apprehension sucked away Susan's breath. "What's happened?"

"Rebecca cut her hand."

"How bad?"

"Not too bad, but she'll need stitches. We're leaving for the hospital?"

"Who's going with you?"

"Jack. Officer Grouchy called him, and he's on the way."

"How did it happen?"

"We were wrapping gifts. I was watching her with the scissors, but there was a piece of glass in the bow box."

"I'm sure it wasn't your fault, Lucy. Are you sure Rebecca's all right?"

"She's not even crying anymore. She's sitting on my

friend John's lap, and he's holding the cold cloth on her finger. The bleeding's almost stopped.''

''John? What's he doing there?''

''He come by to make an emergency Christmas-paper delivery. The children had a couple of surprises to wrap. The officer said it was okay for John to come in if I vouched for him, but he'd have to stay in the room with us.''

''Okay, tell me about the cut.''

''Wait, Susan. Someone's at the door. I think it's Jack. We'll call you after Rebecca sees the doctor.''

''No, I'll meet you at the hospital.''

Susan hung up the phone just as her next patient walked in the door. She'd see her for a few minutes, but not for the full session. Auntie Mom was needed at the hospital.

*4:00 p.m.*

SUSAN AND HER ever-present bodyguard rushed down the hall toward the room where the nurse had directed her. She heard Jack's booming voice before she got there.

''Now, see? That wasn't so bad, and you have a great-looking bandage. I bet Missy Sippen never had a bandage like that.''

She pushed through the half-open door.

''Auntie Mom, you came.''

''Of course I came.'' She hugged Rebecca tightly.

''You're too late,'' Jack said. ''You missed all the fun.''

''It was *not* fun,'' Rebecca corrected him. ''The doctor gave me a shot right here.'' She pointed at the appropriate spot. "And he gave me stitches. I didn't even cry."

Susan hugged her and pulled her pigtail out of her collar. "I'm so proud of you."

Rebecca filled her in about all the details of the stitches. She was still talking when the doctor came in and gave them directions for cleaning the wound and changing the bandages.

"Can you go home with us, Auntie Mom?" Rebecca asked, when the doctor finished his spiel and left them alone.

"I'm afraid I have to go back to work and see a few more patients, but I'll be home early so that I can have lots of time with you and Timmy before you go to sleep."

"Is that one of your patients?" Rebecca asked, pointing at the officer who had accompanied Susan.

"No, this is Mr. Simpson. He's a friend of mine."

"You sure have a lot of new friends lately," she said, shaking her head as if she didn't quite get it. "Miss Lucy says they eat a lot, and they're as messy as Timmy."

Susan stuck her head outside the door to see if she could catch a glimpse of the waiting area. "Where is Timmy?"

"He stayed with Mr. John and one of those friends who keep hanging around our house. He was taking a nap and Lucy didn't want to wake him up, did you, Miss Lucy?"

"No way. Timmy's much too fussy when he doesn't get his nap out."

They started back down the hall and toward the car. "I still can't imagine how a piece of glass happened to be in the bow box," Susan said.

"I'm afraid I have to take the blame for that," Lucy

explained. "I ran out of wrapping paper one day and borrowed some of yours. I had a little present for John's birthday, and I wanted to give it to him that night."

"I remember now. You mentioned you'd come over one day when we were out and used the wrapping supplies."

"Actually, I never got to use the paper, or the bows. The aftershave slipped out of my hand and splintered into a thousand pieces before I could get it wrapped. It took me almost an hour to clean up the mess. You must have smelled it when you came home that day."

"You broke...a bottle of aftershave lotion...that you'd bought for John." Susan's knees grew weak.

Jack's gaze met Susan's in the split second realization hit home. He took off at a dead run. And Susan was right behind him.

# Chapter Fourteen

*5:00 p.m.*

Jack pulled into the tow-away zone, lights flashing and sirens yelling. Susan jumped from the car before the motor died. Hammonds was there. She had to focus on that. Even if Lucy's Mr. John was Darby, Hammonds would protect Timmy.

She raced up the walk, her breath coming in jagged puffs, knowing deep inside her that her logic was faulty. Hammonds couldn't stop Darby. No one could.

Jack beat her to the door. He slammed his hand against the wood paneling as Susan fitted the key into the lock. The key turned, and he shoved in ahead of her, gun drawn.

A string of curses flew from his lips. Susan pushed around him and then stopped dead in her tracks. Hammonds was sprawled across the foyer floor, her face blue, a scarf knotted around her neck.

She opened her eyes, dark circles in her swollen face. "It was Darby," she said, gasping for breath. Jack fell to the floor beside her.

Susan turned away. Her mind shut down, but adrenaline shot through her body, driving her on. "Timmy."

Feet flying, she raced from one room to another, calling his name. "Timmy!" But the house was deathly silent.

Jack grabbed her and held her. "He's not here, Susan. Darby took him, but we'll find him."

Rage consumed her, and she lashed out at the only thing she could reach. She beat her fists into Jack's chest until he took her hands and forced them to stop. He rocked her shaking body against him.

"It was me he wanted. Me!" she cried. "And he can have me. I don't care anymore. Just don't let him hurt Timmy." Her voice was choked with pain and fear. And fury such as she had never known before.

Jack's body tensed, a knot of muscle and resolve. "He can't have you," he said, his voice bitter and hard. "And he can't have Timmy. We will not let a madman win. Not this time."

JOHN JASPER DARBY carried the sleeping child wrapped in a light blanket into his apartment on the edge of the French Quarter. A little sedative powder in the boy's soft drink had worked wonders and made his job so much easier. He'd vowed to put Susan McKnight through the longest day of her life before he killed her, and that day had begun.

He hadn't considered kidnapping in the beginning, had never imagined that Susan would be the kind to want or have children. He'd merely set out to hook up with her friends and discover the best way to engineer his payback.

Finding Lucy Carmichael had been an act of pure luck, though he hadn't thought so in the beginning. A fruitcake, who went around talking to her dead husband as if he were as alive as she was and sitting beside her.

And then there had been Bobby Chambers. He'd been

a tougher shell to crack than Lucy, but he had come around. A few beers and the man would talk.

But his crowning achievement had been finding Maggie Henderson for his first victim. He hadn't intended to kill anyone that day, hadn't even sent his first note to Dr. Susan McKnight. But Maggie looked so much like Susan had that first time he'd met her—seven long years ago—that he'd changed his plan.

Seven years he'd spent locked away, on the say-so of some green psychologist straight out of school. Kelsey and Susan, the Drs. McKnight. They had ruined his life. But they wouldn't get away with it. Kelsey had already paid. Now it was Susan's turn.

His hands itched to wrap around her neck. Maybe he wouldn't even use a scarf this time. Maybe he would do it with his bare hands. He had pretended it was Susan he was killing the night he'd strangled the life from Maggie's beautiful body. But this time it would be a thousand times sweeter. This time it would be Susan, and his payback would finally be complete.

Timmy would deliver her to him.

*Friday, December 24*
*3:00 a.m.*

SUSAN SAT at the kitchen table, waiting for a phone call from Darby. The same way she'd been sitting and waiting for the last ten hours.

"Any news?" she asked, when Jack left the command post he'd organized in the wide foyer, and joined her in the kitchen. She didn't have to hear his answer. His tormented eyes said it all.

"No news." He stopped behind her and massaged her shoulders "And no news is good news."

"I have to believe that. I just wish Darby would call, let us know Timmy's all right."

"Is Rebecca sleeping?"

"Yes, Lucy lay down with her and they both fell asleep."

"She's a real little trouper."

"She is," Susan agreed. "I'm just thankful Lucy and Simpson kept her away from the house until after the paramedics and the ambulance arrived for Hammonds. I tried to keep her in her room and shielded from all this most of the night, but I think she knows something's wrong, something more than your using the apartment to work on a police case."

"Did she ask about Timmy again?"

"No, apparently the fact that he went to spend the night with Lucy's Mr. John is fine with her." Susan shivered, wrapping her arms about her chest. "I can't bear to think that Darby was in my home, playing with the children, but evidently they never saw the monster side of him." She buried her head in her hands. "I just pray Timmy isn't seeing it now."

"No reason to think he is. Darby has no reason to harm Timmy. According to Lucy, they were buddies. Hold on to that, Susan." He took her hands. "Hold on to me. I'll be here."

"Will you, Jack?"

"As long as you need me."

"What if that turns out to be forever?"

Jack ran his fingers through Susan's hair, tangling a curl around his finger and letting the soft tresses slip away slowly. Forever. It was a word he seldom thought of. A word he wasn't sure existed in his world.

"We'll talk about forever when this is over with," he

said. "Right now every hour seems an eternity." It was the only honest answer he could give.

"What happened between you and your wife?"

He dropped to the chair beside her. "That's a strange question to ask at a time like this."

"Not really. You're so supportive, so loving, so good with kids. But she left you. She had to have reasons."

"She did. I'm a cop. You've been with me for ten days. I don't sleep, eat, or make decent conversation when I'm on a case like this. I lose all perspective."

"You're a dedicated detective."

"That wasn't the kind of dedication she was looking for. She wanted a man who was home for dinner at five, who spent Saturday mornings working in the yard, who kept social engagements."

"But she married *you*."

"Yeah, but it didn't take her long to tire of the roller coaster. She jumped off at the first stop, two months before we'd have celebrated our first anniversary. She did the right thing for both of us. I don't have any hard feelings. We just didn't mesh, as you call it."

The phone rang, and Susan jerked to attention. Hands shaking she picked up the receiver. Her hopes plummeted when Casanova asked to speak to Jack. She handed him the phone and went back to the range to start yet another pot of black coffee.

*5:00 a.m.*

LUCY WOKE UP and stared at the ceiling over the double bed where she lay beside Rebecca. "Are you there, Stephen?"

She closed her eyes and waited for a sign. At first there was nothing. Then her heart did the crazy flutter it always did when he came around.

"I made a big mistake. I think you tried to tell me, but I didn't listen. I missed you so much. I just wanted another person to talk to and laugh with. I won't make that mistake again. From now on, I'll check out any man I meet with you before I so much as have a cup of coffee with him."

Rebecca squirmed in her sleep, and Lucy calmed her with a pat. Poor darling. She'd probably rolled over on her cut finger. Lucy waited a second, until she felt Stephen's presence again.

"Take care of Timmy," she whispered. "Watch over him. You were so good with kids, just like the nice detective who's here with Susan. If you have any powers at all, do this one thing for me, Stephen. I wouldn't be able to bear it if I thought I'd brought harm to that little boy."

She waited quietly in the dark. Her heart didn't flutter again, but a warmth seeped into her as if she were cradled in someone's arms. "Thank you, Stephen," she said and brushed a lone tear from her eye. "I knew I could count on you."

Rebecca rolled over. "Are you talking to me, Miss Lucy?"

"No, honey. You go back to sleep. I was just talking to my angel."

"Is he watching over us?"

"Yes, over all of us."

Lucy waited until Rebecca was asleep again. Then she got up and tiptoed back to the kitchen to wait for news.

*8:00 a.m.*

SUSAN OPENED burning eyes that were swollen from the
avalanche of tears she'd finally shed. The living room
was dark, but she could hear voices in the background.
She stretched and checked the clock over the mantel.
She'd only meant to rest a minute, but she must have
fallen asleep.

Sliding her feet back into her shoes, she stumbled to
the kitchen. Jack was the first thing she saw. "Any
news?"

He took her in his arms and held her close, like she
might have done Timmy after a bad dream. "Not yet."

"Did you sleep at all?"

"A quick nap."

"Why don't I believe you?" She hugged him close
and then left the circle of his arms to find a cup for
coffee. "Where's Casanova?"

"He went out to get some food, but he'll be back.
Hammonds' replacement is in the foyer."

"How is Hammonds? Is she in the hospital?"

"She's doing fine. In fact, she apparently said she
wanted to be here, on duty. We have a missing child.
You could have every cop in the city here today if we
needed them."

Susan poured a cup of strong, black coffee.

"You could go back to sleep instead of drinking that.
I'll wake you if we hear anything."

"I'm not sleepy." She dropped to the kitchen chair.
"Why doesn't he call? Or send a note. He couldn't wait
to deliver notes before." Desperation tore at her voice.
She didn't try to hide it. The wait had been too long.

"He hasn't contacted you because the rotten scum is
fulfilling his objective. He wants you to suffer. He's
made sure you are."

Susan's head ached, a dull throb that encompassed

both temples and rode the base of her skull. She massaged the back of her neck.

Jack moved closer and took over the job, digging into her flesh with firm fingers. "He'll have to call soon," he said. "It's Christmas Eve."

"Do you think Darby cares about that?"

"Not ordinarily. But he said you'd be begging him for mercy by Christmas. In order to do that, you'll have to talk to him."

"I'm more than ready to beg right now." All she could think of was Timmy alone with Darby. Was he warm? Was he hungry? Was he asking for her? That was as far as she would let her mind go. To think anything more frightening would destroy her will when she needed it most.

Casanova returned a few minutes later with bagels and doughnuts and a bottle of orange juice. Jack insisted she try to eat, and she picked at a bagel. The bread wouldn't go past the lump in her throat. Besides, her stomach was a lead ball that had no need for food.

"I'd wanted this Christmas to be one Rebecca and Timmy would always remember."

"Don't do this to yourself, Susan. Darby will call. Timmy will be all right. You have to hold on to those thoughts."

Susan studied the long lines in Jack's face and wondered if he really believed that himself or if it was just more cop talk, reassurances used to keep her calm so they could do their job.

The phone rang again. Susan grabbed it. This time it was for the new cop on duty. She took it to her and then went to stare out the back door and into the courtyard.

"I know a little about your father," Jack said, "but you've never mentioned your mother."

"I don't remember much about her. She died when I was three. After that it was just my father and me. He was my life—the Center was his."

"I'm sure he loved you, too. How could anyone not?" Jack caught her fingers in his.

"He did love me, in his own way. It took a lot of years for me to understand that, but I finally did."

"Did you tell him that?"

"Yes, the year before he died. I told him that I loved him."

"So Darby's comment about making peace with your dad doesn't apply."

"No, but he probably heard about the argument my dad and I had when I left the Center and moved to New Orleans. The truth is, I'm a lot like my dad was. It's difficult for me to show my emotions, difficult for me to open up and let people into the private parts of my life."

"Your job is working with people."

"Right. So was my father's. On a professional basis, I'm confident and assured. In my personal life, I've always been a very private person. Cold, some people have said."

"I'd argue that with them. You've opened up to me."

"You are one of the exceptions."

Jack squeezed her hand. "How did your dad die?"

"An apparent heart attack. He died in his sleep at the Center. He had a room on the second floor with a bed and a few personal items, and he frequently stayed there after I left home. No foul play was suspected so we didn't request an autopsy."

Susan got out of her chair and walked to the counter. "I'm sorry you had to miss out on your family Christmas in Abilene, Jack."

"I've missed it before. I'll miss it again. They understand. In fact, my mom would have my hide if I wasn't here with you at a time like this."

"Your mom doesn't know me."

"She knows about you. I talked to her on the phone a couple of days ago. I told her all about you and Rebecca and Timmy. She wants to meet all of you."

"You know, Jack, if there's any good that's come out of this nightmare, it's been the change in my relationship with the kids. This whole ordeal has made me realize how much they mean to me. I couldn't love them more if I had given birth to them."

"I'm sure their mom knew that would happen when she made you their guardian."

"I expect you're right. Carrie was a very smart lady. And fun. Always upbeat and ready to grab the gusto. She had a way of seeing qualities in me I didn't know were there, a lot like you do."

The phone rang again. This time Susan didn't jump for it. Repeated disappointment had dulled her response time.

Jack pushed the phone toward her. "You should be the one to answer."

She lifted the receiver. "Hello."

"Dr. Susan McKnight. You're up early this morning, or did you sleep last night?"

Her heart jumped to her throat. "Darby. Where's Timmy?" Her words alerted every officer in the house.

"He's here with me. He's such a nice, bright boy. Unlike you, he doesn't think Mr. John is crazy."

"Is he all right?"

"He's fine. I have no reason to hurt him, unless of course you don't do as I ask."

"What is it you want me to do?"

"Come to see me, Susan. Alone. I'm telling you now, if you bring the police you will never see Timmy alive again. And you do know I mean what I say. Think of Maggie and Sherry."

"I want to talk to Timmy."

"Of course, he's here at the warehouse with me. Timmy, come over here, son, your auntie mom wants to talk to you."

Trembling, she waited for the little voice to come across the wires.

"Hi, Auntie Mom, are you going to come and get me?"

"Yes, Timmy. Are you all right?"

"Uh-huh, but Mr. John didn't have any Cheerios, so I had to eat his bran stuff. It was yucky. So I need to come home and eat breakfast. Can I have Cheerios and chocolate with marsh'ellos?"

"Yes, sweetie. You can have anything you want for breakfast."

"Mr. John said I was staying with him until Rebecca got her finger fixed. Is it well yet?"

Tears filled Susan's eyes. "Yes, your sister's all well and I'm coming to get you." Her voice broke on the words.

"I'm going back to the loft and play now."

"Be careful, Timmy."

"All right, Dr. McKnight," Darby had taken the phone, but his words were little more than a whisper. "Are you ready to listen and do as I say?"

"Tell me where to meet you. I'll be there."

"Timmy and I are in a warehouse on the river. It's deserted now, but it has a lovely ambiance for this type of rendezvous."

Susan listened to the directions, writing down every

word and then repeating them to Darby so there would be no mistake. When she hung up the phone, her fingers were shaking so badly, she had to use two hands to get the receiver into the cradle.

Jack wrapped a hand around her waist. "Let's get this show on the road, Susan. Casanova and I will draw up the game plan."

"No!"

"This isn't up for debate, Susan. Darby plans to kill you the same way he did the others. We'll stay in the background as long as we can, but…"

"No!"

Jack, Casanova and Hammonds all remained silent, staring at her as if she'd just landed from another planet. She didn't waver. "Darby said for me to come alone if I wanted to see Timmy alive again. I'm following his orders, Jack. I'm a psychologist. This is my specialty. If I don't upset Darby, I can make him listen."

"You don't believe that any more than I do, Susan. If you go in there without backup, he'll kill you and maybe Timmy, too. I'm not about to let that happen. When you walk into that warehouse you'll be wearing a mike, and we'll have the place surrounded."

"Darby might check for wires. And all he has to see is one policeman for him to kill Timmy and me."

"There won't be any wires. Just one tiny microphone, the size of a large pin hole, disguised as part of your clothing. We do this my way, Susan, or you don't leave this house."

Jack had reverted from lover to cop. His voice was stern, his posture straight and formidable.

She met his gaze unflinchingly. "If something happens to Timmy because a cop shows his face before he's free, I will never forgive you. *Never.*"

"I don't blame you a bit. Now get dressed while we work out the details."

Casanova stepped in. "You'll need to wear a shirt with white buttons up the front. If you wear a coat or jacket, it has to be opened so that it never covers the front of the shirt."

Jack and Casanova returned to the foyer where three other cops were already huddled over a card table, drawing lines and making notes.

"I'm coming, Timmy," she whispered as she ran up the stairs to dress in a white shirt. "I'm coming to get you."

# Chapter Fifteen

Susan slowed to a stop in front of a deserted warehouse that sat on the banks of the muddy Mississippi River. The windows were boarded, and obscene graffiti was smeared across every wall. Not a place for the faint of heart to visit. Leave it to Darby to find it.

And somewhere inside the daunting gray building, Darby was waiting for her. Darby and Timmy. She wouldn't have to look for them. Darby would find her. Whispering a prayer, she opened the car door and stepped outside. A gust of wind slapped her in the face, and she pulled her coat tighter as she dodged the debris that littered the walk.

A step at a time, cool and calm. Jack had assured her his plan would work, but the closer she came to the door, the more doubt and fear engulfed her mind. They were not dealing with an ordinary man.

The first order of business was to get Timmy outside. The moment he was safe and out of Darby's sight, a policeman would pick him up. After that, she was supposed to maneuver so that Darby faced the east side of the building. Jack and Casanova had already contacted the owner of the building and gotten a detailed description of the interior. Their rescue plan was in place.

Susan had her own objectives. Get Timmy out of the building, and get Darby to confess to killing Sherry and Maggie. She had to make certain he never had the opportunity to take another innocent life.

Darby would probably be in no rush to kill her. He obviously got his kicks from her suffering, so he would drag this out as long as possible. If at any point she thought either she or Timmy was in immediate danger, she was to say Jack's name loud and clear. Cry wolf and clear a path so the men in blue could save the day. On paper, it had looked foolproof. Now, a few steps from putting the plan into operation, she knew a million things could go wrong.

She stepped inside the door of a building that smelled of mold and rotting wood. The interior looked pretty much as Jack had told her it would, except that it was much colder and far darker than she'd expected. There were few inner walls, only rafters and bare boards and one rickety stairwell that led to a second-floor loft. She scanned the room.

"Darby, it's Susan. I'm here to meet you." Her voice carried through the empty building, coming back to her in ghostly echoes. She longed to turn and run, to escape the dark shadows and the fear that squeezed the air from her lungs. But somewhere in this dark building a killer waited, and he had Timmy.

"Come in, Susan. Timmy and I were waiting for you."

The voice came from behind her. She spun around, and the nauseating odor she'd come to associate with fear touched her nostrils.

"Auntie Mom, what took you so long? Mr. John took me out back by the river. There was big boat out there, but I got cold so we came back in."

Timmy ran to her and she wrapped him in her arms, holding him against her.

"Don't hold me so tight," he complained, squirming from her embrace. "You're hurting me."

Reluctantly, Susan released him from her arms but held on to his hand.

Darby stepped closer. "I think she's glad to see you, Timmy. Now, why don't you go back to the loft and play while your auntie mom and I have a talk?"

"No, Darby. That's *not* the deal."

Timmy looked up at her. "Are you mad at Mr. John because he took me to see the boat?"

"No, I'm not mad. It's just that it's too cold in here. I don't want you to get sick." She took a deep breath to steady her nerves. Her gaze locked with Darby's. "I want Timmy to go and sit in the car while we talk."

"Timmy would rather be inside with us, wouldn't you, Timmy?"

Timmy looked from Darby to Susan, confusion shadowing his blue eyes. "I'm ready to go home," he said, tugging at Susan's hand.

"We'll go home soon. *Mr. John* and I have a bargain we need to seal. I've kept my part of it. I came for you by myself. Now I expect him to keep his."

Darby laughed, cold and mocking. "Fine, go ahead and sit in the car, Timmy. Run now, before I decide not to be so agreeable."

Susan squeezed his hand extra tight. "Go to the car and wait for me. Hurry. And don't come back in here. It's too cold. You don't want to be sick for Christmas."

"Is tonight the night Santa comes?"

"Yes, sweetie. Tonight. Now run. I'll see you in a few minutes."

"Okay. I have to do what you say and be real good,

so Santa will leave me toys. Goodbye, Mr. John. Thanks for keeping me, but you sure eat yucky cereal.''

Susan didn't realize she was holding her breath until Timmy ran through the door into the sunlight and she felt the burn of dank air filling her lungs. The rest would be easy. Timmy was safe, and Jack could hear her every word.

''It looks as if it's you and me, Susan. Together, at last.''

She struggled to sound calm. ''I know you're angry with me. I can understand that.''

Darby shook his head. ''Don't start that psychological routine on me. I was with your father for years. I've heard it all. The problem is I'm much better at playing with people's minds than either you or your father ever were.''

''You are a very smart man, Darby. That's why I think you'll turn yourself in and go back to the hospital. If you kill me, the police will track you down and take you to jail. It will be far worse than the hospital, and I don't think you'll do anything to hurt yourself.''

''I'll do what I want. I have, all my life. I do whatever I choose to whomever I choose. But not because I'm crazy the way you told the judge I was. It's because I'm *evil*. Just plain evil, though neither you nor your father could accept that. I've always known exactly what I was doing.''

Susan's blood ran cold. She took a step backward, but Darby reached out and grabbed her wrist. ''I knew what I was doing, but that doesn't mean I forgive you and your father for locking me away in that godforsaken Center where I was treated like some poor sick soul.''

''We wanted to help you, Darby. I still do.''

''You are going to help me.'' He stuck his other hand

into his pants pocket and pulled out a bright purple scarf. He smiled as he shook the silky folds lose and twirled it in her face. "When I kill you, I will feel so much better. Just like I did when I killed your father."

"You didn't kill my father. He died in his sleep."

"That was thoughtful of me, don't you think? I saved my medicine for months, those little white pills they gave me to make sure I didn't cause them too much trouble. When I had enough, I requested that your father have dinner with me."

"And you put the pills in his food, no doubt knowing about his heart condition." Anger shook the voice she'd been determined to keep smooth.

"Of course. Now don't interrupt me. You're spoiling my story." He tightened his grip on her arm until she winced in pain. "I accidentally knocked over my glass of water. When Kelsey jumped up to avoid the spill, I sprinkled the ground-up pills into his coffee. So easy. So easy. He just went to sleep never to wake up again."

"That was a long time ago, Darby. You didn't know what you were doing. Let me take you back to the hospital. They'll help you."

He twisted her arm behind her. "I'm not going back to the hospital. I should never have been there. I'm not crazy. Don't you understand yet?"

"If you hadn't gone to the hospital, you would have gone to jail."

"No, I would have walked free. They couldn't have pinned those murders on me. They had no proof. *You* were the one who sentenced me to live my life in an institution, you and your father."

Susan forced her mind to concentrate. She tried to turn so that Darby would, too. Right now he was facing north. But he yanked her back around to face him. "I know why you want to hurt me, Darby. But why Maggie, why Sherry?''

"I hadn't planned to kill Maggie. I had moved to the French Quarter to seek out your friends, to get to you through them. I met Maggie in a nightspot. She looked so much like you did when I first met you that I couldn't help myself. And once the game had begun, I had to play it through to the end. That's what we're doing today.''

"A game that you controlled completely.''

"Exactly, but you weren't suffering nearly enough. You were laughing and riding around in carriages, flirting with that cop who came sniffing around your door every night. So I had to find the one thing that would tear the heart from you before I wrapped this pretty silk scarf around your neck and strangled your life away.''

"Kidnapping Timmy.''

"Yes, another stroke of genius on my part. One look at you today, and I knew my plan had worked. Only I didn't designate Timmy. Originally I'd thought it would probably be Rebecca. But when she cut her hand, everything fell into place. So easy. It was all so easy.''

He jerked her closer, until her body pressed against his. His eyes glazed over, and the veins in his neck and face popped out, blue rivers against the red of his flushed skin. This was the side of Darby that Maggie and Sherry must have seen in the seconds before he strangled the life from their bodies.

"I want one thing from you before I kill you, Dr. McKnight." He spat out her name as if it were a curse. "I want you to admit that you were wrong. I am *not* crazy.

"Admit it, Susan. Admit I'm not crazy.''

She tried to jerk from his grasp, but he twisted her

arm until pain shot through her body in paralyzing stabs. She'd learned enough. It was time to call in the troops.

She stamped on his foot as hard as she could and fought to twist away, to make him face the east wall. But he was much too strong. She couldn't pull free.

In the struggle, the scarf fell from his hand. She kicked it away, and that was when she noticed the pistol in his hand. Fear consumed her. She'd waited too late to call for help. Even if Jack and the other police officers rushed in now, the gun would still go off, the pistol that was all but touching her left temple. He would kill her and possibly Jack as well.

"So long, Susan." He pointed the gun at her head and cocked it.

She gave one last twist, trying desperately to escape his grasp. The bullet cracked through the silence, echoing like rolling thunder in her brain. A crippling pain slammed against her chest, and she fell to the cold, hard floor.

## Chapter Sixteen

"The game's over, Darby. You lose."

Susan jerked to attention at the sound of the voice. The hard, rough tone was as unmistakable as Jack's ho, ho, ho. Or was she hallucinating? She tried to move, but her legs wouldn't budge.

Finally, she twisted until she could see her feet and legs. They were under a body, Darby's. A jade handle stuck out from between his shoulder blades, but he wasn't dead. A couple of policemen were helping him up and into a pair of handcuffs. For once, he was silent.

Jack stooped down beside her and cradled her head in his arms. "Are you all right?"

"Am I alive?"

"You are unless the fall killed you."

She rubbed her aching wrist. "Where did you come from?"

"The loft. When Darby pulled the gun, Casanova and I had to move quickly. By that time we'd already given up on your being able to get him to face the opposite wall, so while you kept him talking, we crawled across the beams and took up new positions. I took the loft. Casanova took that beam behind you."

Susan looked up. The loft had to be at least twenty feet above the floor. "You jumped from there?"

"I didn't have a lot of choice. Besides, I planned on Darby breaking my fall. After listening to him talk, I decided it could be the first useful thing he'd ever do in his life."

"Was that a knife in Darby's back?"

"No." This time it was Casanova who answered. She turned as he stepped from the stairs that led to the loft. "The handle was attached to a dart. Mine."

"Where were *you?*"

"Do you see that beam up there?" He pointed to a spot high over their heads.

Susan's mind was still reeling. "Wait a minute. You threw that dart from the top of the warehouse. What if you'd missed your mark?"

"It can't happen."

"Don't believe him," Jack said. "He was off by at least an eighth of an inch." Jack helped Susan to her feet, steadying her in his arms.

"I thought I'd waited too late to call you," Susan said, her mind still in a state of semishock. "How long had you been in the loft?"

"Since before you came into the building. There was no way I was leaving you or Timmy alone with Darby."

"That wasn't the plan."

"It was *my* plan, and I'm the detective in charge." He hugged her against him. "Now are we going to stay here and argue all night, or do you want to go home? It's Christmas Eve, you know, and Timmy and Rebecca are waiting for you."

Susan blinked, and a tear of pure joy escaped. "I'm ready to get out of here, Detective. But, for the record, it's been one hell of a ride."

*Friday, December 24 10:00 p.m.*

SUSAN SAT on the couch and stared into the fireplace and the fiery glow of dying embers. The last few days would live in her memory forever, a bitter reminder of the power of evil, but she wouldn't let John Jasper Darby rob her or the children of the precious moments of the present.

She was still amazed that Rebecca and Timmy had come out of this virtually unscathed. Attribute it to the resilience of childhood, and the fact that Darby for some unknown reason had not wanted to hurt Timmy. He'd even managed to keep Timmy from seeing him when he'd attacked Hammonds.

*Within the hearts of the vilest of men, there is always something they hold sacred.* A quote from Dr. Kelsey McKnight. Apparently, Darby's sacred area was children. As far as Timmy was concerned, he and Mr. John had experienced a wonderful adventure. Except for the bran cereal, which was *yucky.*

Still, sleep had been slow in coming tonight for either of the children. It was Christmas Eve, a magical evening, and anticipation had them flying high. Now they were finally nestled all snug in their beds and dreaming pleasant dreams, no doubt. If not visions of sugar plums, then at least reindeer and Santa and wonderful surprises they'd find under the tree Jack had brought them. She only hoped they wouldn't be too disappointed when Santa didn't fulfill their wishes exactly as they'd requested.

She wasn't really worried about Timmy. He would probably be thrilled with the tricycle and the toy train, especially after she assured him they could get a puppy later. She wasn't so sure about Rebecca. She had her heart set on something that only she and Santa knew about. If Jack was in on the wish, he had been as secretive as Rebecca.

Detective Jack Carter, a man of many talents. Her heart warmed, thinking of him. She'd wanted this Christmas to be special for the kids. As late as this morning, the chances for that had been almost nonexistent. Tonight, she doubted anything could spoil the day.

The nightmare was over, and most of the thanks had to go to Jack. She glanced at the clock over the mantel. She hadn't heard a word from him since the rescue. She wasn't surprised. He was busy wrapping up the investigation, making sure the case against Darby was airtight. All or nothing, the only way Jack knew to operate.

Still, it would have been nice to see him or at least talk to him tonight. Now she'd have to wait until tomorrow to tell him Merry Christmas. And wait to tell him that she loved him.

No strings, no promises, he'd said, but she knew she could never settle for that, not for herself or the children. She hoped he couldn't either.

She wanted strings, rings and the ties that bind. Living with Jack wouldn't be easy. They were opposites in so many aspects of their lives, but vive la différence. Now that she'd been on the roller coaster, she had no desire to return to her life of steady walking on level ground.

She'd learned a lot about herself and about Jack in a very short time. She'd made her choice. The rest would be up to Detective Santa and the magic of the season.

*10:30 p.m.*

"SCORE ONE MORE for the good guys," Casanova said, sticking his head into Jack's cubicle. "I just watched the evening news, and the reporters who were lambasting the police a couple of nights ago are now calling us heroes.''

''Heroes who had a lot of luck on our side. Maybe even an angel, if you believe Lucy Carmichael.''

''Tomorrow I may doubt, but tonight I believe,'' Casanova said, propping himself against the door frame. ''When Darby disappeared with Timmy, I wouldn't have bet you a warm beer that we'd see him alive again.''

''Susan never gave up hope.''

''No, the dragon lady's got guts. But when Darby pointed that gun at her head, I thought she was history. Obviously, you did, too. I've never seen a man turn that shade of white and still be breathing. Come to think of it, why aren't you over at the McKnight house tonight?''

''I've got some paperwork I need to catch up on.''

''Paperwork? You're kidding me. You've got a beautiful woman waiting, and it's Christmas Eve. And in case you haven't noticed, the beautiful woman is crazy about you.''

Jack leaned back in his chair and put his hands behind his head. ''She is now. I'm the hero. But what are the chances it would last? A woman like her. A man like me. I've seen explosives with a better chance of blending peacefully.''

''You wouldn't get my vote for most compatible couple of the year, but it could happen. Look at…Beauty and the Beast.''

''That's a fairy tale.''

''So, you'd just walk away without trying?'' Casanova shook his head. ''I'm glad I didn't know you were such a coward today when I was depending on you to take that leap from the loft. If you hadn't taken Darby out before he figured out where the dart came from, he'd have fired on me. I'd have been an easy target, perched up there on the beam.''

"This is not a matter of bravery. It's a matter of good sense and doing what is right. If I get involved with Susan, I also get involved with Rebecca and Timmy."

"So? You love kids."

Jack tapped the eraser end of a pencil against the arm of his chair. "Especially those two. I didn't mention this, but that first night when I showed up at Susan's house in the Santa outfit, Rebecca told me what she wanted for Christmas."

"Yeah?"

"She wants a husband for her auntie mom. She reminded me of that again the other night."

"Apply for the position. You could do a lot worse."

"I've seen my résumé. I'm not husband material."

"So settle for a fling. I do it all the time. A few months dating a cop who's never around when they need him, and they dump me. I get over it."

"You just don't get it, do you, Casanova? It's not just Susan and me who would suffer when the inevitable breakup happens. It's the kids. And they've already had enough loss in their lives without going through it again. The best thing I can do for all of them is to just close out the case and walk away. They'll forget me soon enough. Susan will go back to her original theory of situational attraction, her term for falling for the cop in charge. For all I know she has already."

Casanova walked over and shoved a stack of clutter to one side of Jack's desk to make some sitting space. "I think you're the one who doesn't get it, Jack. You're underestimating the dragon lady. She's not about to go running when the going gets tough. If you don't know that by now, she's too good for you anyway."

Casanova reached in his shirt pocket and pulled out the jade-handled dart, his new good-luck piece. He took aim and hurled it at the target. It hit its mark, right in the center of the bull's-eye. "I'm out of here, old buddy. I've got a new girl waiting who thinks I'm the best thing since microwave popcorn." Casanova retrieved his dart and headed toward the door. "Merry Christmas and all that jazz."

"Yeah, sure. You, too," Jack answered without looking up. "Merry Christmas, Casanova."

Jack sat at his desk, in no mood to go home and spend Christmas Eve alone. Today, in that warehouse on the river, he'd been to hell and back. That split second when Darby had pulled the gun from inside his jacket and pointed it at Susan, Jack had known his first taste of hopeless terror.

Fortunately, his training had taken over, made him focus on what had to be done, helped him coordinate his movements with Casanova's, the way they'd done so many times before in tough situations. But, even now, just thinking how close he'd come to losing Susan to a bullet, he felt the terror all over again.

He wanted Susan more than he'd ever wanted any woman in his life. Cared for her enough that he could make himself walk away if it would be best for her and for Rebecca and Timmy.

Or was Casanova right—was he only kidding himself? Was he just too much of a coward to take a chance on love with the beautiful dragon lady?

Jack picked up a dart from his desk and hurled it at the target, not bothering to aim. He walked closer to get a better look. Son of a gun. A perfect bull's-eye. He grabbed his jacket and headed home. It had been days since he'd had a good night's sleep. No wonder he couldn't think straight.

*Saturday, December 25*
*8:00 a.m.*

"AUNTIE MOM, get up. Santa came, and he left toys."

Susan opened her eyes and rolled over. Timmy was standing in the door, his eyes wide and shining. "Are you sure?" she asked.

"Yes. I peeked in the living room. I saw a choo-choo train."

Susan threw her legs over the side of the bed and grabbed her robe. "Well, then we better wake Rebecca and go see what else Santa left. First, I need a hug, though. A big Christmas hug."

Timmy ran over and threw his pudgy arms around her neck. "Ho, ho, ho. Merry Christmas."

Susan held him tight. "Merry Christmas, Timmy."

They went and woke Rebecca, and the three of them marched into the living room together. The morning was nearly perfect, filled with laughter and hugs and brightly wrapped packages. Susan had so much to be thankful for that she was loath to acknowledge the gentle ache of disappointment that lodged in her heart. Jack still hadn't called.

She made excuses in her mind. Jack was a cop first. Any number of emergencies might have come up. He'd warned her that when he was on a case, he forgot everything else.

The excuses were reasonable, but none of them eased her mind or lightened her heart. It would only have taken a minute to call and say Merry Christmas. Everything

Jack did, he did with a purpose. He hadn't called because he had chosen not to.

Finally, it was Rebecca who put words to her fears. "Do you think Detective Santa forget about us?"

"I don't think so, sweetie. I imagine Mr. Jack's just very busy. Do you like the doll you got from Santa Claus?"

"She's very pretty."

Rebecca did a poor job of hiding her disappointment. Susan pulled her onto her lap. "Sometimes Santa can't bring everything you want, Rebecca, but if you tell me what it is, maybe I can buy it for your birthday. It's not long until March."

"No. You can't buy it."

"Why don't we go out in the kitchen and cook breakfast?" she said. "It's Christmas. We can have anything you guys want."

"Not yet," Timmy said, riding his trike around in a circle. "I'm waiting for Detective Santa. He's bringing my puppy."

"I don't think so, Timmy, but I told you we can go shopping for one next week."

"He'll bring it," Timmy said, "when he gets through working."

Susan felt a new stab of pain to her heart. Detective Santa. Yesterday's hero. He had promised them magic, and they had all believed. Now they were all suffering the pangs of disappointment and plunging back into reality.

No matter, they were all alive and well. Jack had given them that, and she would never forget his determination and bravery over the last few days. He was what he was, a cop who loved the excitement of living on the edge. He was bigger than life, a thrill a minute, and for a while he had carried her along on his roller coaster.

If she never saw him again, she'd still be glad she took the ride. But she would miss him for a long, long time. Susan got up, determined to brighten her mood for the children's sake. It was Christmas.

"Let's take that tricycle out to the courtyard, Timmy, and you can show me how fast you can go. Rebecca, why don't you come too? Put your new doll in the carriage and take her for a walk in the sunshine."

"THIS TURKEY LOOKS wonderful," Lucy exclaimed, "golden brown and perfect. When and where did you learn to cook like this?"

"This morning and from a cookbook, so don't brag too soon. You may have to eat your words along with a cardboard-tasting bird."

"I don't think so. I've already taste-tested the sweet potato casserole and the cornbread dressing. They're divine." She smacked her lips. "Should I pour milk for the kids?"

"Please. I'll get the iced tea as soon as I finish with this salad, and could you check the rolls? They smell like they're burning."

Lucy opened the oven, and more of the wonderful scents of Christmas cooking poured out into the room. "They're not burning, but they're ready. I'll put the butter on the dining-room table. This will be so festive."

They had just said grace when the front doorbell rang. Rebecca jumped up and ran toward it as if she'd been shot from a cannon.

"It's Detective Santa," Timmy yelled, climbing out of his booster seat.

It wasn't. It was Officer Hammonds, who was still

bruised, but back on duty. Susan invited her in and asked her to stay for dinner.

"I couldn't do that," she protested. "I just came by to bring a little something for Rebecca and Timmy. I hope you don't mind."

"Of course not."

"Okay, are you ready, Rebecca and Timmy? You are about to become honorary police officers." She leaned over and pinned a miniature badge on each of them, replicas of the ones she and Jack carried.

"Now we're just like Mr. Jack," Rebecca whispered in total awe.

"Is he here?" Hammonds asked. "I don't want to keep you from your dinner, but I'd like to tell him Merry Christmas."

"I haven't seen him today," Susan answered, determined not to let her disappointment show. The look in Hammonds' eyes told her she'd failed.

"He's not here now, but he's coming," Rebecca said. "I know he is. He wouldn't forget about us on Christmas." Her lip quivered ever so slightly, and Susan wrapped an arm around her.

"Are you sure you don't want to join us for dinner?" Susan asked. "We have plenty."

"No, I'm off duty at three. We'll have our family dinner then. I just wanted to see the kids again and wish you all a merry Christmas. Yesterday, I thought…"

"I know." Susan hugged her warmly, fighting back the tears that burned in the corners of her eyes. "We are very lucky. We owe a lot to you and the entire police department."

"Especially to Jack," Hammonds said. "He gives every case two hundred percent, but I've never seen him get that personally involved before. He's a special guy, Susan, and he needs you.''

"He'll have to decide that.''

They finished their goodbyes and went back to the table. Lucy raved about the food, but Susan and Rebecca only picked at theirs. Detective Santa might have gone on to his newest case, gone on with his life, but he'd left three people behind who would miss him for a long, long time.

"Auntie Mom,'' Rebecca said, poking her potatoes with her fork, "what would happen to Timmy and me if we were too much for you to handle? Would you give us away?''

Susan all but choked on a bite of stuffing. She put down her fork and met Rebecca's gaze. "Of course I wouldn't give you away. Wherever did you get such an idea?''

"You said it. I heard you one day on the phone. You said you didn't know how you were going to manage us by yourself.''

"Oh, sweetie. Have you been worried about that?'' Susan scooted her chair close to Rebecca's.

"We don't want to leave here,'' Rebecca said.

Susan swallowed a lump the size of a grapefruit. She put her arms around Rebecca and held her close. "I loved your mother very much, Rebecca. And she and your father loved you. But that's not why I love you and Timmy. I love you because you're in a special place in my heart. I would never, ever, ever, give you away or let anyone take you away from me. Do you understand?''

Rebecca hugged her back. "I'm glad, but I still hope I get what I asked Santa to give me for Christmas.''

"Are you sure you don't want to tell me what that something is?"

"No, I think Detective Santa should tell you."

"He may not be coming today, Rebecca. He's a very busy man."

"He'll come, Auntie Mom. Don't worry. He'll come."

The children finished eating and went back to their new toys, but Susan lingered over a second cup of coffee. She hadn't eaten much lunch, but she had managed to finish off a piece of Lucy's pumpkin pie.

"Stephen loved pumpkin pie," Lucy said. Her eyes took on that faraway look they always did when she talked about Stephen.

"You must have loved him an awful lot," Susan said.

"I still do. Love never goes away. It hangs around forever. Like a warm fuzzy feeling in your heart."

"Maybe that's only if the man you love loves you back."

"I don't know." Lucy turned around and looked out toward the courtyard. "What is that noise? It sounds like a little yapping dog."

Susan jumped up just as Timmy came tearing by her. He swung open the back door and a small golden retriever pranced through the door as though he owned the place. Jack was right behind him.

"It's my puppy." Timmy said. He got down on his all fours and the animal licked him on the face. "He likes me," Timmy said. "Thank you, Detective Santa."

"You're welcome, big boy. Merry Christmas."

"Ho, ho, ho," Timmy said, and then he was off following the puppy down the hall.

Glad as Susan was to see Jack, she still had reservations about the gift. "That's a retriever, Jack."

"Right. A wonderful dog for boys."

"They get very big. And this is a small apartment."

"That's the other thing we need to talk about."

"The size of my apartment?"

"Sort of. Look, Susan, I have a present for you, but I want to do this right. Let's go into the living room."

"I can leave and come back later," Lucy offered. "If you'd like I can take the kids for a while. That way you two could exchange your Christmas gifts in private."

"No, you should stay, Lucy. You're practically part of the family. And Rebecca *has* to be here. This is her surprise, too." He winked at Rebecca, and she clapped her hands.

"I knew it. I knew it," she sang. "I knew you wouldn't forget my surprise. You might not be the real Santa, but you're the best secret Santa in the whole world. I told Missy Sippen that."

"This isn't another big-animal surprise, is it?" Susan asked dubiously.

"As a matter of fact, it is. Don't get alarmed yet. Just walk into the living room and sit down in the big chair."

Susan did as she was told. Everybody gathered around for the show. Now she was really getting nervous.

"I don't ever plan to do this again, so I want to do it right." Jack dropped to his knees in front of her and took her hands in his. "Susan McKnight. I'm asking you to be my wife. I'm no bargain, but you already know that. But I love you and Rebecca and Timmy, and I'll be the best husband and uncle dad that I can possibly be." He looked up at Rebecca. "Am I doing this right?"

She bent down and whispered in his ear. "Where's the ring?"

"Right, the ring. It's here in my pocket somewhere. I had to call a lot of jewelers to find one who would open for me on Christmas Day." He fished in his pants pockets and pulled out a gold and diamond engagement ring. He held it up, ready to slip it on Susan's finger.

"If you don't say yes soon, Susan, I'm going to lose my nerve."

"Yes. Yes. Yes!"

This time she didn't try to stop the tears. They rolled down her cheeks. Jack slipped the ring on her finger and pulled her to her feet.

"Merry Christmas, Susan. The first one of many, many to come."

"Merry Christmas, Jack. For forever."

Lucy cried. Rebecca clapped her hands. Timmy played with his new puppy. And Jack kissed his bride-to-be.

*9:00 p.m.*

REBECCA AND TIMMY were in bed, and Susan and Jack were finally alone. Jack added another log to the fire and threw two pillows to the carpet in front of the hearth. Susan joined him on the floor.

"I think we'll need a bigger place," he said. "Your apartment is nice but it's already bursting at the seams."

"So that explains the retriever."

"They're gentle, and that one looked at me with pleading eyes. I couldn't leave him alone on Christmas. Besides, the children could use a yard, too. One big enough for playing catch. And the house should have sidewalks out front for riding tricycles and skating."

"You've given this some thought."

"Half of the night. The other half I spent getting up the nerve to ask you to marry me."

"Does marriage frighten you that much?"

"No, the possibility of failing at marriage for the second time did. I had to convince myself that this time it would last forever. I owed that to you and the children and to myself."

"What convinced you?"

"You, and something Casanova said last night. Basically, he said you weren't a quitter and insinuated that I should know that from seeing you in action the last few days. He was right. You are not only brave, smart and beautiful, but you never once gave up when faced with a killer. I knew if you love me the way I love you, we'll find a way to work out our differences and stay together."

She snuggled against him. "Just try to get rid of me, but I do have a few questions."

"Shoot."

"I haven't been able to figure out how Hammonds managed to survive the strangling when none of Darby's other victims did."

"A lot of luck. He caught her off guard and hit her over the head with something heavy. No one is sure what. Anyway, when she passed out from the blow to the head, he thought she was dead. He grabbed Timmy and took off before he'd tightened the scarf enough to fully cut off her oxygen supply."

"And what about Gabriel? Did he ever talk to you?"

"A little. He remembers calling Sherry and getting no answer. He knows he went to her house after that and found her strangled body. Beyond that, the facts are foggy. He doesn't remember taking the scarf from around her neck and tucking her into bed, but the prints at the scene indicate that's probably what happened. And the pattern of bloodstains indicates he fell and hit his head against the bed railing, probably while trying to get her under the covers.'' Jack kissed a spot at the nape of her neck. ''Any more questions?''

''Yes. There's still Bobby. How did he fit into all of this?''

''I'd still be working on that myself if Bobby hadn't finally decided to talk. He said Darby started hanging out at the casinos and bars that Bobby frequented. He convinced Bobby to choose a couple of names out of your files and use the information to his own benefit. He chose Gabriel and Carolina Taylor.''

''Good choices. They both had plenty of money and lots of skeletons in their closets.''

''Exactly. Lots of blackmail ammunition.''

''And I was convinced he was just a hardworking young secretary.'' Next time she'd be a lot more careful in employee selection. ''Obviously, Gregory didn't bite.''

''No. According to Bobby, he didn't really care who his wife slept with as long as he could do what he wanted. Gabriel didn't buy into blackmail either, but he offered to pay Bobby big bucks if he'd snoop on Sherry. Bobby took him up on the offer. He followed Sherry after work, and that's how he knew she was seeing her partner, and how he knew they flew out to Chicago together.''

''And Bobby shared all of the dirty facts with Darby.''

''Right again. Darby wanted to hurt you, and he planned to do that by making you feel responsible for the murders he committed.''

''So it could just as easily have been Carolina he killed?''

''Or anyone else you knew, even Lucy. Instead, he used Lucy to find out the details of your life, to get into your house, and to become close to your children. I'm sure he even took her keys long enough to have a set made for himself after we caught him at the window.''

''That's why he was able to walk in that night and leave the wrapped package on Rebecca's bed.'' Susan shuddered. ''He said he was evil, and he proved it over and over. Even with my father. But I'll be thankful forever that he didn't hurt Timmy.''

''And that he didn't kill you.'' Jack buried his mouth in her hair.

Susan nestled in his arms. ''I have one question left.''

''What's that?''

''Remember that first night when you came to my house in a Santa Claus suit? You weren't really moonlighting at the mall, were you?''

''Of course not.''

''Then why were you dressed like that?''

''The truth?''

''The truth.''

He nibbled her earlobe. ''I'm Santa Claus,'' he whispered. ''Didn't I bring you everything you wanted for Christmas?''

''Not yet,'' she whispered, ''but if you hurry, we still have time.'' She found his lips with hers and kissed him, passion already simmering inside her.

He stood and swooped her into his arms. ''Have you been a good little girl?'' he whispered, starting up the stairs to her bedroom.

''Not as good as I plan to be in the next few minutes. What do you have to say about that, Santa?''

He smiled, the devilish, devastating smile that signaled the roller coaster was about to take off. She held on tight.

''Ho, ho, ho,'' he said, his voice low and sexy, and raspy with desire. ''Merry Christmas.''

And indeed it was.

Lost & Found

*All new...and filled with the mystery and romance you love!*

**SOMEBODY'S BABY**
by Amanda Stevens in November 1998

**A FATHER FOR HER BABY**
by B. J. Daniels in December 1998

**A FATHER'S LOVE**
by Carla Cassidy in January 1999

It all begins one night when three women go into labor in the same Galveston, Texas, hospital. Shortly after the babies are born, fire erupts, and though each child and mother make it to safety, there's more than just the mystery of birth to solve now....

Don't miss this *all new* LOST & FOUND trilogy!

Available at your favorite retail outlet.

HARLEQUIN®
*Makes any time special* ™

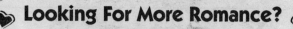

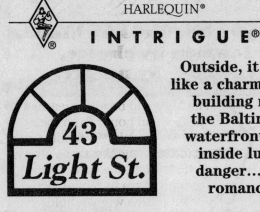

# They're brothers by blood, lawmen by choice, cowboys by nature.

**THE COWBOY CODE**

The McQuaid brothers learned justice and honor from their father, the meaning of family from their mother. The West was always in their souls, but now it's the past they have to reckon with. And three women hold the keys to their future.

*Don't miss this exciting new series from three of your favorite Intrigue authors!*

## McQUAID'S JUSTICE
**Carly Bishop**
January 1999

## A COWBOY'S HONOR
**Laura Gordon**
February 1999

## LONE STAR LAWMAN
**Joanna Wayne**
March 1999

Available at your favorite retail outlet.

**HARLEQUIN®**
*Makes any time special* ™

# Dangerous, powerful and passionate...

## THE
# AUSTRALIANS

Stories of romance Australian-style, guaranteed to
fulfill that sense of adventure!

This January 1999, look for

# *Her Outback Man*

## by **Margaret Way**

Logan Dangerfield, head of one of Australia's most affluent
families, had severe doubts about Dana Barry's motives.
Offering comfort to Logan's niece kept Dana on his cattle
station, but could she hide the fact that Logan was the only
Outback man she had ever loved?

*The Wonder from Down Under: where spirited women win
the hearts of Australia's most independent men!*

Available January 1999
at your favorite retail outlet.

# HARLEQUIN®
*Makes any time special* ™